The Unmasking

Emmeline did not know why Lord Charles was laughing at her, calling her, "You little innocent . . ." but she did know that it infuriated her on this, her wedding night.

"Don't you dare laugh at me, you . . . you. . . ." Her eyes flashed, and before he realized her intention, she slapped him across his cheek.

Emmeline had never hit anyone before, and had no idea what would happen next. She was not long in finding out. With one hand he caught her wrist, while with his other he grabbed her chin and fiercely yanked it up.

"You want to know why I married you? Well, I'll tell you. I married you because I have to produce an heir!" he roared, and released her so suddenly that she fell back against the chaise.

Was this the tender gentleman who had won her trust? Was this the handsome lord who had won her heart? How had she ever given her hand to him—and what could she do now as he claimed the rest of her . . . ?

The Reluctant Bride

① SIGNET REGENCY ROMANCE (0451)

Amorous Escapades

- ☐ THE UNRULY BRIDE by Vanessa Gray. (134060—$2.50)
- ☐ THE DUKE'S MESSENGER by Vanessa Gray. (138856—$2.50)
- ☐ THE DUTIFUL DAUGHTER by Vanessa Gray. (090179—$1.75)
- ☐ THE RECKLESS GAMBLER by Vanessa Gray. (137647—$2.50)
- ☐ THE ABANDONED BRIDE by Edith Layton. (135652—$2.50)
- ☐ THE DISDAINFUL MARQUIS by Edith Layton. (145879—$2.50)
- ☐ FALSE ANGEL by Edith Layton. (138562—$2.50)
- ☐ THE INDIAN MAIDEN by Edith Layton. (143019—$2.50)
- ☐ RED JACK'S DAUGHTER by Edith Layton. (144880—$2.50)
- ☐ LADY OF SPIRIT by Edith Layton. (145178—$2.50)
- ☐ THE NOBLE IMPOSTER by Mollie Ashton. (129156—$2.25)
- ☐ LORD CALIBAN by Ellen Fitzgerald. (134761—$2.50)
- ☐ A NOVEL ALLIANCE by Ellen Fitzgerald. (132742—$2.50)
- ☐ THE IRISH HEIRESS by Ellen Fitzgerald. (136594—$2.50)
- ☐ ROGUE'S BRIDE by Ellen Fitzgerald. (140435—$2.50)

Prices slightly higher in Canada.

Buy them at your local bookstore or use this convenient coupon for ordering.

NEW AMERICAN LIBRARY,
P.O. Box 999, Bergenfield, New Jersey 07621

Please send me the books I have checked above. I am enclosing $_____ (please add $1.00 to this order to cover postage and handling). Send check or money order—no cash or C.O.D.'s. Prices and numbers are subject to change without notice.

Name_____

Address_____

City_____ State_____ Zip Code_____

Allow 4-6 weeks for delivery.
This offer is subject to withdrawal without notice.

The Reluctant Bride

Irene Saunders

A SIGNET BOOK

NEW AMERICAN LIBRARY

NAL BOOKS ARE AVAILABLE AT QUANTITY DISCOUNTS WHEN USED TO PROMOTE PRODUCTS OR SERVICES. FOR INFORMATION PLEASE WRITE TO PREMIUM MARKETING DIVISION, NEW AMERICAN LIBRARY, 1633 BROADWAY, NEW YORK, NEW YORK 10019.

Copyright © 1986 by Irene Saunders

All rights reserved

SIGNET TRADEMARK REG. U.S. PAT. OFF. AND FOREIGN COUNTRIES
REGISTERED TRADEMARK—MARCA REGISTRADA
HECHO EN CHICAGO, U.S.A.

SIGNET, SIGNET CLASSIC, MENTOR, ONYX, PLUME, MERIDIAN and NAL BOOKS are published by New American Library, 1633 Broadway, New York, New York 10019

First Printing, December, 1986

1 2 3 4 5 6 7 8 9

PRINTED IN THE UNITED STATES OF AMERICA

*In Loving memory of Ray,
my husband and dearest friend*

One

The Marquess of Millford's size was impressive. So impressive, in fact, that at times he had been described unkindly as obese. Excessive consumption of good wine and good food, with little or no exercise, had increased his girth to a point where he could sit only in the most commodious of chairs and couches, and he was so plagued with gout that walking was frequently a painful, if not impossible, proposition.

Seated in a massive wing chair behind a desk that had been his father's, he squinted a little as he struggled to read the fine feminine hand of a letter that had arrived this morning. Coming as it did from the widow of his old friend Lord Grantley, it brought back memories, both happy and sad. It would seem she had found a document he and her first husband had executed some fifteen years before.

His quiet chuckle caused the loose folds of his cheeks to quiver, and he closed his eyes as though to better see into the past. He remembered it as if it was yesterday. It was back in 1803, and England was at war once again with France, but this had had little effect on two middle-aged men of rank and wealth. They'd been to Newmarket, picked the winner, by Jove, and had imbibed a little too much of the grape in celebration. They fell to commiserating with each other, he on the fact that he had only one son to succeed him, and Grantley because he had no sons sat all—only three daughters, his last hope of a son having vanished just two days ago when the third girl had been born.

Like the old friends they were, they hit upon the idea of his son's marrying one of Grantley's daughters, and they put it in writing there and then, and signed it on the spot.

By the sober light of day, neither man had given the matter another second's thought, or so the marquess had believed—until Grantley's widow had uncovered the agreement in a drawer of old papers she was about to discard. Or at least that was what she wrote in her letter.

He stretched out a chubby hand, reached for a sheet of his crested notepaper, and started to reply to the lady who, having remarried, was now Lady Barrow. Nice enough woman, very pretty if his memory served him, but not nearly good enough for old Grantley. He was the best!

AT THAT MOMENT Lord Charles Carruthers, the marquess's only son, was on his way to visit his father. The marquess's health had not been of the best in recent months and as he was extremely fond of his often irascible father, he had tried of late to spend more time at the family home than had previously been his custom.

Charles, at the age of thirty-three, was still unwed, a fact that was causing his illustrious parents grave concern. His disinclination to tie the knot with any of the lovely young things they frequently pushed in his direction was, according to them, a complete disregard of familial duty.

He halted his curricle in front of the house and, giving the reins to his groom, ran lightly up the steps as the door swung open to reveal the elderly butler, Bentley, trying hard to keep a smile of welcome from his usually impassive face.

"Her ladyship is not home yet, milord, but his lordship is in the bookroom. Shall I announce you?"

"No, thank you, Bentley, you need not trouble. I'll just go right in and surprise him," Charles replied. "Good to see you again."

Crossing the large hall swiftly, he tapped lightly on a door and entered without waiting for a response. He had covered more than half of the rich Axminster carpet before his father looked up from the letter he was composing.

"What the . . . ? Charles, my boy!" The marquess made to rise, but then sat down hurriedly with a grimace. "Forgive me for not getting up but my leg's been deuced uncomfortable of late."

Father and son clasped hands warmly, and Lord Millford waved impatiently at the armchair close to the desk. "Sit there where I can see you."

The old, watery blue eyes missed nothing, from the black curly hair tamed into the very latest mode, to the high—though not exaggeratedly so—collar points, to the coat and waistcoat, cut of the finest cloth with a fit that only Weston could achieve.

He gave a nod of approval. "It's hard to believe, looking at me now, that I once cut as fine a figure as you do. Getting old is purgatory, my boy. Where did you spring from this time? Your mother'll be delighted to see you. She gets lonely when there're just the two of us."

"I'm on my way north, sir, to the Grahams' place for a couple of weeks' shooting." He raised a questioning brow. "I had thought that Margaret would still be here with the children."

He was not entirely displeased at the absence of his sister and her offspring. Although he held his sister in the highest regard and there had always been a genuine warmth and affection in their relationship, her children were in need of a tighter control than either she or her husband seemed capable of exerting.

His father gave him a knowing look. "And you were glad to find them gone this last sennight, I don't doubt. Her ladyship loves her grandchildren, but she takes to her bed for a week after they leave." He sighed heavily. "Your sister is increasing again, you know." He frowned as he remembered a distasteful subject. "And, speaking of grandchildren . . ."

He stopped as Bentley came in with refreshments—a propitious interruption for Charles, as his father was about to embark on what was to him a most irritating topic of conversation.

The taste of his best Madeira made the marquess feel a mellow glow and put thoughts of grandchildren momentarily out of his mind, but as he cleared a space for his glass on the massive mahogany desk, his eye fell on the letter he had been about to write before his son's welcome interruption.

"Do you remember Lord Grantley? Had a fair-sized place up in Yorkshire with good hunting and superb grouse shooting on the moors nearby. We saw a lot of each other in the old days, but it may have been a bit before your time," said the marquess.

"I'm sure I met him, sir, but I was barely out of leading strings. Didn't he pass on a few years ago?" For some reason Charles felt vaguely uncomfortable, as if something unpleasant was about to happen.

His father set his glass carefully down on the inlaid surface of the desk. "He did, more's the pity, two years since, and his widow, Barbara, was no sooner out of mourning than she met up with a gamester, real rum sort by all accounts, and married him."

Charles was wondering what his father's sudden interest in an old friend's affairs might be and how it affected himself, but experience had taught him patience where his father was concerned. The marquess loved to milk a story to the last drop. This time, though, Charles didn't have long to wait.

"Take a look at this letter I received from the former Lady Grantley. I was just preparing a reply when you arrived." His lordship's sardonic tone had a hint of malice in it. He held out two pieces of paper and Charles reached over to take them, mildly curious as to their content.

As he watched his son's face change from curiosity to amazement and finally to an expression of disdain, the older man's wrinkled eyes held a glint of mischief, which was quickly concealed when Charles gave him a suspicious look.

"My lord," he began with some irritation, "I assume that the document is a forgery, but I cannot comprehend the purpose in sending it to you at this time."

Lord Millford shook his head emphatically. "It's no forgery, Charles. That's my signature, and I can also vouch for that of Grantley. We wrote it all right."

With a now unreadable expression on his handsome face, and eyes narrowed to prevent their giving away a spark of feeling, Charles spoke in an unusual, dangerously soft tone of voice. "If the pair of you signed such a document fifteen years ago, I can only think that you were both in your cups at the time, my lord."

The old man chuckled gleefully. "It's not easy to fool you, my boy. You guessed it right away. We were both jug-bitten, and the next morning we held our sore heads and laughed about it. But we'd signed the agreement and apparently he hung on to that piece of paper." A glimmer of an idea was forming in the back of his mind. The girls' ancestry was impeccable, so why not? Both parents were exceptionally good looking, so he doubted that the daughters could have turned out to be horse-faced. "Don't look so worried, Charles. We didn't specify which daughter was to become your bride, or when. He had three, you know."

"Sir, if you mean to imply that I have any obligation, legal or moral, to honor a marriage contract entered into by two besotted fools . . ." Charles rose to his feet, glaring at his father, and flung the offending piece of paper on the desk.

"How dare you speak of me in that tone, sir!" the marquess thundered, his face turning red with anger. "I have given you every opportunity these past half dozen years and more to choose yourself a suitable bride. But none are good enough for your lordship! There've been any number of suitable, handsome chits, including the daughter of a duke, more than willing to receive your attentions. But what do you do? You ask them for the odd dance, take them for a drive once or twice, then drop them the minute they show a preference toward you."

Charles had started angrily in the direction of the door, but turned back at his father's verbal assault. "My dear papa," he said icily, his own temper now under careful control, "allow me to make myself clear. I have no intention of remaining single, but I will marry whom I wish, when I choose to do so, and it will not be one of the simpering young misses that my mother and her friends persist in introducing to me, nor the daughter of a duke who seeks a loveless married state in order to pursue her cicisbei."

Choked by fury, the marquess struggled to get to his feet, but failing miserably he dropped back into the chair and fixed a steely eye on his son. "You have not yet reached a stage where you can tell me what you will and will not do, my lord! I can't stop you succeeding to my title when I'm gone, and I know you have the small property in Warwickshire that your uncle left you, but just you mark my words," he vowed, his face flushed and his eyebrows meeting menacingly, "I'll give you twelve months to get yourself a suitable bride and if you disobey me you'll live on that property for the rest of your life, on whatever income you can derive from it. This estate is not entailed, nor are the London townhouse and the other properties you've been attending to on my behalf, and, damme, I'll leave them to your cousins unless you do your duty by this family." His fist crashed down on the desk in emphasis.

Charles received the ultimatum without a flicker of an eyelid. He was angrier with his father than he had been for many years, and he did not intend to allow him to control his life, but he had noted the high color of the older man's complexion, and knew the danger to his health any further aggravation might be. Although he had planned a quiet evening with his parents, he decided to avoid the possibility of further contention.

"I will not be home for supper, sir, but will see you tomorrow morning before I leave," he said quietly, and with a courteous bow he left the room.

The butler was in the hall, and Charles stopped to have a word with him.

"Bentley, the marquess is a trifle out of sorts. I'd appreciate it if you could think of some excuse to go into the bookroom and see that he's all right," he murmured softly. "You might also be sure Mother takes a look at him when she comes home."

For once, Charles regretted making the stopover. After a mediocre meal at a nearby inn, preceded by a scolding from the marchioness who blamed him for upsetting his father, he retired much earlier than was his habit.

The next morning, when ready to take his leave, he was informed that the marchioness was breakfasting in her bedchamber and expecting him to stop by before he left.

She looked older, sitting up in bed with a deep rose wrap around her shoulders and her silver hair covered with a lace sleeping cap, but age had not dimmed her sparkle one wit.

"Leaving so soon, my dear?" She sighed a little and held out her arms. "Don't drive that curricle of yours too fast on those narrow roads, and enjoy your shooting."

He kissed her cheek affectionately. "I'll be back in about a fortnight, Mama, but should you need me in the meantime, you know where to reach me."

He found his father in the bookroom again.

"Leaving already, Charles?" he asked, disappointment showing in the droop of his massive shoulders. He looked a trifle unwell and, as Charles had expected, showed no desire to speak of their quarrel of the previous day.

"I'm afraid so, sir, but I'll be back this way in a fortnight with plenty to tell you about the hunting." It was not in his nature to leave without apologizing for his rudeness, but he knew it was the best thing to do on this occasion. Threats had been made in the past and not carried out, but a reference at this time to his latest ultimatum might make his father feel compelled to abide by it.

"Wonder if you'd do me a favor, my boy. Grantley's place is not far from the Grahams'. Would you mind stopping by and giving Lady Barrow this letter, with my best regards? It wouldn't be a half hour out of your way." The marquess held out the letter to which he'd just affixed his seal, and smiled in a beguiling fashion.

It was just about the last thing Charles wanted to do, but he couldn't upset his father again. He suspected that an attempt was being made to ensnare him, but he knew that he was capable and experienced enough to extricate himself from any difficulties that might arise.

"Of course I will, sir," he responded with alacrity. "Then when I return here I can tell you what Lady Barrow had to say, and bring you the latest *on-dits* with regard to the Grantley family."

"Don't forget to give her my regards, and watch out for Lord Barrow. He'll probably try to get you to play cards, and do so by all means if you wish, but keep a sharp eye on him. There used to be some odd rumors circulating about Barrow."

With a firm handclasp they parted. The marquess slumped back into his chair when he was alone once more, and hoped the threat, which he'd no intention of carrying out, might make Charles at least take a second look at the Grantley girls. If nothing else, he'd managed to get him to go there, and the rest would be up to Lady Barrow and her rake of a husband.

Two

There was a chill in the air, and the shadows cast by the old oak trees had deepened. Emmeline had stayed out longer than she intended. Sitting on the edge of the brook, her boots at her side, her bare feet playing with the minnows and tadpoles as they darted through the icy clear water, she had no sense of the passage of time. She could feel the cold hardness of the limestone rock against her back and smell the faint woodsy fragrance of moss and dead leaves.

With eyes half closed, she dreamed of the day when she would leave Grantley Range and make her own way in the world—escaping from the silly prattle and constant scoldings of her mother and older sister, and the viciousness of her stepfather.

She was playing truant again. Clad in breeches and shirt, she had ridden off early this morning astride her colt, Thunder, whom—much to her mother's and her sister Agatha's disgust—she had helped raise from birth.

Such tomboyish escapades had been forbidden some twelve months ago, and she knew the consequences would be severe if she were found out. But her stepfather and his groom were away for a few hours, her sisters had gone on a picnic with a neighboring squire's daughters, and her mother had taken to her bed with a megrim, so discovery was most unlikely.

As for the grooms and stable hands, Jack, the head groom, might scold her, but every one of them would cover for her if necessary. Jack was about the age her father would have been and had been her only friend and confidant since her father had passed away. He was a short, wiry man with a broken nose, the result of a youthful fall from a stallion, and skin burned copper by exposure to the elements. Together with her father, he had taught Emmeline to ride almost before she could walk, much to her mother's dismay. From berating her soundly whenever she took foolish chances and receiving her sincere, tearful apologies, a rare affection had sprung in the tough ex-jockey's heart for the plucky little girl.

The sun was now past its zenith, but Thunder was well rested, so heaving a sigh, Emmeline climbed into the saddle and headed for home. Leaning low over Thunder's neck, she let the colt have his head and they raced back toward the house as though the devil himself was chasing them.

The Grantley property, situated as it was just south of York on a tributary of the River Ouse, wasn't difficult for Charles to find. Having once agreed to deliver his father's letter, he had felt the responsibility weighing heavily upon him and decided to execute his commission first before proceeding to the Grahams'.

When he saw the house from a distance, located as it was on a slight rise, and surrounded by what appeared to be extensive gardens, he felt a pang of sympathy for his father's late friend. It was a pity, he thought, that such a handsome estate was entailed and could not have been passed on to one of the daughters. Suddenly, his thoughts were interrupted by the nearby thundering of a horse's hooves and his eye caught the figure of a girl on horseback racing madly across the fields.

As Emmeline neared the entrance gate, she was startled to see a curricle approaching from the opposite direction, drawn by a very fine pair of grays, and driven by a smartly dressed, darkly good-looking man. There was something about him that caught her attention and made her stare in fascination as they drew closer, despite her wish not to be seen. As her eyes met his penetrating gaze, she felt a strange uneasiness. She knew for a certainty she had never met him before, and yet she felt as though she knew him.

With a slight inclination of his head, he held back to allow her to enter first. Taking a deep breath to relieve the sudden tightness in her chest, she discourteously turned her head away, hoping he might not recognize her again, completely forgetting that her mane of pale gold hair would provide easy identification.

Letting her horse slow to a trot so that he could cool down before they reached the stables, Emmeline found herself oddly possessed by the urge to steal another look at the stranger. Glancing over her shoulder, she found him staring curiously after her and quickly turned back.

As Charles drove down the drive toward the front entrance of the manor, he could not help wondering which Grantley daughter the blond tomboy might be. That she was a daughter of Lord Grantley he was quite sure, for she had the very same startling blue eyes and golden hair his father had described his friend as having. Though he thought her somewhat lacking in good manners, Charles could not but admire her handling of such a spirited colt, and noted ruefully that she had aroused more interest in him than any other female had for many months. Just curiosity, he told himself firmly. He would have liked to have followed her around to the stables, but then he himself would have been guilty of bad manners. Reluctantly tearing his eyes from her retreating figure, he brought the grays to a halt in front of the house.

Inside the stables, Jack silently handed Emmeline the old muslin print gown she'd discarded earlier in the day, and took Thunder to the back of the stables. Slipping into an empty stall, she dropped the gown over her shirt and breeches, the high neck and long sleeves of the dress successfully concealing the other garments.

She almost overbalanced in her haste to pull off her riding boots and put on the dark slippers she took from the pocket of the gown. Then, as soon as the boots were hidden, she ran quickly to the back of the house and moved silently through the servants' entrance and up the back stairs to her bedchamber.

THE DRAWING ROOM into which Charles was shown on presentation of his card was elegant, if somewhat faded and worn, and it was not long before he heard a light footstep in the hall.

Lady Barrow greeted him a little too warmly, almost as though he and not his father had been a friend of her late husband. Anxious that she not jump to any wrong conclusions, Charles hastily gave her the letter which was the reason for his call. With a flutter of eyelashes, she begged to be excused while she broke the seal and read the contents, toward the end of which she nodded slowly, then broke into a wide-eyed smile. He immediately became suspicious of what his father might have put in the letter.

She gave an exaggerated little sigh. "I can quite understand what happened," she said, in a voice a shade too high and girlish for her forty-odd years. "You men all become more romantic after a glass or two of wine, and Lord Grantley was so very concerned about the future of his little girls."

It seemed to Charles that she included herself in the latter group. Acknowledging her remark with only a faint flicker of a smile, he rose. It was late in the afternoon and he'd best find a decent inn for the night as he'd not be able to get to the Grahams' before dusk.

Lady Barrow rose also, and a look of alarm flickered in her eyes before she asked with concern, "Surely you're not leaving, my lord? My husband will be here momentarily, and I know he would be most insulted if you were not to accept our hospitality and spend the night at the Range." She fluttered her eyelashes at him once more.

For a fleeting moment Charles felt as though he was playing a part in some carefully rehearsed charade, and had almost made the wrong move. Then he heard footsteps in the hall once more, heavy ones this time, hurrying toward the drawing room.

As though on cue, a tall, thin older man entered, dressed in a beige coat of light broadcloth with a white linen shirt beneath a white cravat, quite fashionably tied. Soft moleskin trousers topped the man's gleaming boots. Charles noted with not a little contempt that a great deal more money was being spent on his lordship's attire than that of Lady Barrow, who was dressed in a green muslin gown several years outmoded.

Lord Barrow gave a questioning look toward his wife, who made the introductions. They were both so insistent that he stay, it seemed easier to acquiesce than to think up a plausible excuse, so Charles allowed himself to be persuaded.

IT WAS REGRETTABLE that the man in the curricle had seen her. Emmeline was most curious as to who he could be. Since Grantley Range was located so far from London, male visitors to the house were rare, with the exception of older men her stepfather brought home to play cards. The stranger would surely be asked to stay to dinner.

She gave some thought to the notion of saying she was sick and unable to eat, but rejected it as too unbelievable. She was never ill, and if she were to miss dinner she'd be starving before breakfast tomorrow. Also, she couldn't help wanting to take another look at him. She felt her cheeks flush at the admission, and put her cool hands to her face. What was the matter with her? She was behaving just like Agatha!

But what if he said he'd seen her riding astride and dressed in breeches? In that case she'd miss dinner and get a whipping besides. She could try willing him not to stay, but doubted her willpower was strong enough.

When Mary, the chambermaid, came with a message from her mother to wear her good white satin and pearls tonight, she knew that it was no use.

There was insufficient hot water for everyone to bathe at the same time, so she washed very thoroughly in the small bowl of cold water Mary had brought. Hoping the odor of horse had been removed completely, she splashed her face and arms with some rosewater she'd been saving for just such a day.

Her hair was straight, the color of palest spun gold, and so thick it took hours of curling rags to turn into ringlets, so she decided to braid it and twist the braids at the nape of her neck as her mother's abigail had done for Agatha's birthday party last month. After she finished she could still feel on her neck the tendrils of hair that had escaped the braids, but it really didn't look bad.

There was nothing she could do about her dark complexion from spending all her time outdoors. Agatha and her mother were forever deploring her lack of looks, and telling her it was not considered pleasing to expose her skin thus. But it did make the pearl necklace seem to glow all the more and gave an added sparkle to her large, sapphire-blue eyes, which were dark-lashed and wide-spaced under arching, sooty brows.

To those who had never known her father, she appeared like a changeling at the side of her black-haired mother and sisters.

It had taken a long time to get ready and it was fortunate that she and her younger sister, Charlotte, were not usually expected to go into the drawing room before dinner. She met Charlotte on the stairs, and went directly to the dining room, arriving just in time to slip silently into the seat her mother indicated, opposite their guest.

Agatha, the older sister, had been placed at the man's right hand, and was giggling and flirting with him so much that Emmeline thought he might not even notice her, but secretly hoped he would. Lady Barrow had lent Agatha the services of her abigail, and she looked magnificent in a rather obvious way. Her black hair was dressed high on her head, with several wispy ringlets seeming to have escaped to trail enticingly around her ears, and her dress, though the white of purity, was cut rather low for a young unmarried woman, and revealed more than a hint of swelling breasts.

"Emmeline, Charlotte, say good evening to our guest, Lord Charles Carruthers. His father was a close friend of your father's." Lady Barrow introduced her two younger daughters.

Charles's eyes twinkled, and a lazy smile twitched at the corners of his mouth. "I believe Lady Emmeline and I have already met, though her attire was somewhat less formal," he drawled with fashionable indolence. "We arrived at the gates at almost exactly the same time this afternoon."

There was an ominous silence at the table, and

Emmeline's face went white, her eyes blue pools of fear.

"Emmeline," Lord Barrow's voice thundered down the table. "If you were out riding again in those breeches, you may leave the table and go to my study. I'll see you there after we finish dinner."

She pushed back her chair to obey her stepfather, but at that moment Charles rose also and addressed his host. The lazy, indifferent manner of a man about town had disappeared completely at the sight of Emmeline's frightened face.

"Sir, if foolish words carelessly spoken by me are cause for punishing this young lady, then I must regretfully take my leave immediately lest my thoughtless tongue cause even more pain."

Lady Barrow looked appealingly at her husband, who also left his seat. "Forgive me, my lord," he said, with a threatening glare in Emmeline's direction. "We so rarely have a guest at table that I forgot my manners. Emmeline, you may sit down and resume your meal."

She took her seat once more, but Charles remained standing. "Unless I am assured that this young lady will not be punished in any way, I cannot in all conscience remain," he said with quiet finality.

Lord Barrow forced an oily smile. "I assure you, Emmeline's conduct is forgiven on this occasion, my lord," he said soothingly. "Let us commence our meal, and perhaps later you will join me in a hand of cards?"

Charles inclined his head gravely and resumed his seat.

The ugly scene had cast a gloom over the table that was difficult to dispel, however much Lady Agatha and her mother might compete for their guest's attention. They giggled and simpered until Emmeline wanted to scream at them, but she carefully kept her eyes down for most of the time and concentrated on her food.

On the two occasions when she did look up, Charles's eyes met hers and he smiled at her reassuringly. She would have liked to thank him, but didn't dare.

Lord and Lady Barrow's ambition was to see one of the girls marry advantageously, and provide a means, both socially and financially, by which they could reenter the society they had each enjoyed many years before. To this end they had been encouraging Agatha to entertain their guest, but when he seemed somewhat more taken with Emmeline, they changed their tactics.

When dinner was over, Lady Barrow ushered the girls into the drawing room, leaving the men to their port and cigars.

She spoke soothingly to her oldest daughter. "It would appear that his lordship has a partiality to Emmeline, so we must encourage him in this. Your time will come, Agatha. You and Charlotte had best leave with me."

Agatha looked venomously at Emmeline as she started to leave the room, and Emmeline made as if to follow them, but her mother put out a restraining hand.

"You stay right here, my girl, until your father brings in Lord Charles. Then he'll make an excuse and leave the two of you alone. Just make the most of it, as I believe he'll be leaving in the morning, but if you play your cards right, he'll be back."

Not daring to disobey, she sat on the edge of a chair and was nervously biting her bottom lip when the two men entered.

Behind Charles's back her stepfather glared threateningly at Emmeline, then said, "Please excuse me for a moment, I must find my wife and have a word with her," and hurried out of the room, closing the door behind him.

With a look of disgust at their crude manners and lack of regard for their daughter's good name, Charles strode to the door and opened it wide, then he returned to where Emmeline waited with some trepidation.

He took one of her hands in his. "Please accept my apologies for the discomfort I caused you at dinner, Lady Emmeline," he begged. "I'm sure you know I had no wish to cause you pain and distress."

She smiled slightly. "Thank you, sir. It was kind of you to take my part," she said. This was the first time she'd been left alone with a strange man, and she was suddenly overcome with shyness.

"I think you must have inherited a great deal more from your father than your golden hair and sapphire eyes," he remarked drily. "Did your mother not yet teach you to simper and giggle?"

She was unaware of the dimples that suddenly appeared in her cheeks when she smiled. Then her expression turned serious again except for the twinkle in those very blue eyes. "I believe those subjects will be included with the dancing lessons, sir," she answered gravely.

"Tell me," he asked with some amusement, "is a stroll in the garden their next suggestion?"

"I'm afraid I really don't know, my lord. You see, you're the first man who ever preferred me to Agatha," she said with unusual candor. "Mother didn't have time to tell me what I should or should not do."

He touched the tip of her nose with his finger. "You're delightfully honest, little one. Don't lose it when they try to bring you out, will you?"

"Honest is not what mother calls it, my lord," she said, a little breathless at his touch. "I don't think I'll lose it, because it would seem I can't help it no matter how angry they become."

Within her admittedly limited experience, Emmeline found him quite the most beautiful man she had ever met. The immaculate cut of his swallow-tail jacket did nothing to hide the broad, muscular shoulders, and at more than six feet in height he towered over her stepfather, with whom there was, of course, no comparison. His black curly hair appeared slightly windblown, but Agatha had told her once, when in an unusually expansive mood, that there was, in fact, such a style carefully arranged to suit current fashion.

He had seemed indifferent and bored with the attentions of her sister, and had listened to her with eyes half closed below his bushy black eyebrows. Now, however, the clear, silvery gray eyes were regarding her intently, and she was sure they twinkled with an inner amusement quite unlike the slightly supercilious smile he had shown Agatha at dinner.

"I could not help but admire your splendid seat on a horse. Who taught you to ride like that?" he asked.

"Our head groom and my father, Lord Grantley, taught me. And my father didn't mind my riding astride in breeches. He said sidesaddles were dangerous and should be banned," she declared with emphasis.

Charles considered the statement carefully. "I wouldn't go so far as that. To ride sidesaddle at the pace you were setting today would be suicidal, I'll admit, but most young ladies proceed at a sedate enough pace to be in very little danger. Do you not agree?" he asked with some amusement.

In her vehemence she showed a sparkle and passion not heretofore apparent, and an attractive flush appeared on her cheeks. "I'd sooner give up riding altogether than become one of those namby-pamby females who pay more attention to their escorts than to their horse," she snorted angrily.

In case her anger was in part occasioned by the grin he couldn't conceal, he hastened to reassure her. "Please don't take me amiss, my lady. I have nothing but admiration for your ability to handle a lively horse. It would seem that your father took you for the boy he always wanted, and in that I cannot fault him—"

"How could you know that?" she interrupted sharply. "You said at dinner that you'd never met him."

"Regretfully, I did not meet him," he agreed. "But my father spoke to me at length of their friendship of many years. That's how I knew you favored him not just in looks."

Her eyes shining with pride, she said, "Thank you, my lord. It is the finest compliment you could pay me."

He had taken a seat across from her as they conversed, but now he rose.

"My ultimate destination is a little to the north of here and can easily be reached in less than two hours," he told her. "I regret I cannot go riding with you, but know it would only put you further out of countenance with your stepfather. If I delay my departure until noon, would you condescend to show me the stables in the morning?" he inquired, with what seemed to Emmeline to be quite breathtaking charm.

Her smile lit her face, and the blue eyes twinkled with mischief. "Of course, my lord. It would be my pleasure to accommodate you. What time would your lordship suggest?" she asked with exaggerated formality.

He considered carefully, knowing that Lord Barrow would likely wish to play cards into the wee hours of the morning. "If I may breakfast about nine, I think we could arrange a rendezvous for, say, ten o'clock. What do you think?"

She showed her pleasure with the reappearance of the two delightful dimples. "Ten o'clock it is, sir."

Reluctantly, she rose to leave, and he escorted her from the room, wishing her a good night as she started to climb the stairs, both of them completely aware of at least two pairs of hidden eyes watching their movements with considerable interest.

* * *

EMMELINE WAS GRATEFUL that when she had attained her eighteenth year, her mother had decided she should have a bedchamber to herself instead of sharing with her younger sister. She needed a few minutes alone to think about the odd way her heart seemed to flutter when Lord Charles took her hand in his, and to understand the breathlessness she felt each time she thought about meeting him again in the morning to show him around their stables. It would be her first assignation with a man, other than one of the neighbors' young sons, who caused no strange feelings in her breast.

He'd looked at her as though he really cared how she felt and wanted her to be comfortable in his company. The way he'd defended her at dinner had been quite wonderful, and made her feel like a real-life maiden in distress and he her knight in shining armor come to rescue her. If only it could be true and this warm, cared-for feeling could be with her always.

Her much-needed solitude was not to last, however. There was the sound of a soft footstep outside her door, and then her mother swept in, arms outstretched.

"Emmeline, my precious! Tell your mama all about it, everything he said and everything he did after we left you alone together," she gushed, seizing her daughter in her arms and clutching her to her bosom in the first embrace Emmeline had received from her in two years. "How unfortunate we did not realize he would become enchanted with you instead of Agatha."

Emmeline managed to wriggle out of her mother's clasp and, stepping back out of reach, began to take off her gown. Part of her longed for her mother's affection, but instinct told her there was little love behind this show of maternal feeling.

Lady Barrow was not to be outdone, however.

"Come now, my dear, let Mama help you, and then

when you're ready for bed we can have a lovely coze." She pushed aside Emmeline's stumbling fingers and helped her out of first her gown, then the considerably worn petticoat, remarking, "I can see we shall have to send for the seamstress to make you some new gowns and things. It won't suit to have a fine man like his lordship coming to call on you, and you looking like a chit fresh from the schoolroom in her sister's old clothes."

"Mama, he's not coming to call on me!" Emmeline protested, despite her secret wish that he might. "He was just being kind because he thought he'd got me into trouble."

"And you assuredly would have been in trouble if he hadn't threatened to leave, my girl." The harsh note Emmeline was accustomed to hearing returned to Lady Barrow's voice, reflecting her earlier annoyance at her daughter's escapade. "As soon as he's gone, I'll have the maids find all those awful breeches you wear and take them and burn them. Then we'll see if you'll defy your father and mother!" she snapped, giving Emmeline a cruel pinch.

Emmeline wanted to say that she wasn't defying her father, just her stepfather, but knew it would only anger her mother still more, so she pulled her nightgown over her head and slipped quickly into bed.

"Not so fast, young lady." Her mother pulled back the covers and hauled her unceremoniously out of bed again and over to the dressing table. "He's going to see you in the morning. We heard him say as much. What do you think your hair will look like if you don't put it up in curling rags tonight?"

This time Emmeline dared to protest. "But Mother, please! I'm too tired. I'm usually in bed long before this."

It was much later than her usual bedtime, and Lady Barrow affected a sweet tone once more.

"I know you're tired, but it won't take long if I help you," she said soothingly. "And tomorrow he'll see how attractive you really can be with your hair in ringlets like a young lady."

There was no help for it, thought Emmeline, and half an hour later she climbed into bed again, knowing she'd sleep restlessly with those awful knots tied all over her head. How she hated having been born a girl, she thought angrily, and not for the first time. Then she realized, to her amazement, that it was no longer true. Despite the discomfort, she was glad now that she was a girl.

But sleep was not to be granted Emmeline just yet, for no sooner had her mother left the bedchamber than the door was flung wide once more and Agatha stormed in. She marched over to the bed, grasped Emmeline by the shoulders, and shook her until some of the curling knots came loose.

"You disgusting little thief! You deliberately set out to steal him from right under my nose, with your pathetic whining when Papa was about to give you a much deserved whipping."

"I did no such . . ." Emmeline started to say, when Agatha released her shoulders suddenly and drew her arm back, but the intended blow was deflected by Emmeline's arm. Though younger, Emmeline was much more athletic than Agatha and within minutes she had grasped both Agatha's arms and held them firmly to stop any more attacks on her person.

She couldn't stop the screeching emanating from Agatha, however, as the older girl proceeded to call her every bad name Emmeline had ever heard, and a great many more she didn't know the meaning of.

Her attempts to placate her sister couldn't be heard above the hysterical threats, and Emmeline finally got out of bed once more, still carefully restraining the hands and arms anxious to wreak vengeance, and pushed Agatha out of the door. Then she leaned against it, turning the key in the lock, and with a weary sigh sank down on top of the covers.

"IT WOULD SEEM your mama has exerted not a little of her influence since the last time we were together," Charles murmured when they had finally been allowed to leave the house and were making their way along the path leading to the stables.

Breakfast had been an ordeal for Emmeline. For the first time in many moons, the whole family had assembled together, instead of her mother and sisters sleeping late and breakfasting in bed. As a rule, she waited in her bedchamber until she heard her stepfather leave the dining room, then ate a substantial breakfast alone and wrapped more food in a serviette for her lunch.

This morning, however, Lady Barrow had come into her bedchamber just as she was dressed and about to go down. Taking one look at Emmeline's old muslin gown and tangled, curled hair, she had ordered her to remove that "rag," and had selected a gown more suitable, in Emmeline's opinion, for making afternoon calls than for visiting the stables.

Twenty minutes later, smarting from her mother's pinches, with her hair brushed into tight ladylike ringlets and one of her mother's lace shawls around her shoulders, she had been allowed to accompany Lady Barrow to the dining room. The frown she had received from both parents when she helped herself at the sideboard to a plate piled high with baked ham, braised kidneys, smoked fish, eggs, and bread and butter almost, but not quite, took away her appetite.

Wearing her over-bright smile, Lady Barrow had carried on a continuous conversation with their guest, seemingly unaware of her husband's reticence. She was unused to seeing him at this hour of the morning, and did not know his reserve was not usual, but caused by the considerable amount of money he had lost to Lord Charles at the card table the night before.

Emmeline, however, had guessed at the reason for his despondency, and was secretly very pleased. She was still sore from her mother's earlier disapproval, and hated the doll-like appearance that had been forced upon her, even to her rosy cheeks induced by Lady Barrow's cruel fingers.

After mumbling a greeting to Lord Charles and seeing the look of amusement on his face, her cheeks had become even pinker, and she had spent the rest of the meal with her eyes on her plate, which she proceeded to empty in a quietly systematic manner.

It had seemed an eternity before the meal ended and she was sent upstairs once more to make repairs to her appearance before returning to the drawing room to meet with his lordship. Any hopes she had harbored that he might be waiting alone were dashed when she heard her mother's too-sweet tones coming from that room. There was nothing she could do save enter and wait for his lordship to make the next move.

This he did with considerable alacrity, taking her arm and steering her in the right direction, while her mother giggled in a girlish way and her stepfather made insinuations as if they were leaving for some kind of tryst.

"I'm s-sorry, my lord," Emmeline stammered, so embarrassed by their behavior that she couldn't even talk properly.

He waited until they were hidden from view, then turned her toward him, gently lifting her chin to make her look at him.

"There is no need for you to apologize for your family," he said sternly. "And as for your appearance, you actually look much better than you think, although I have a strong temptation to dip your head in the horse trough when we get to the stable and wash out those awful, unfashionable curls."

Her laughter was at first a little nervous, but soon it became so infectious that he couldn't help but join in, and the ice was completely broken.

"You've no idea," she said between gurgles, "how awful it is to sleep with your hair tied in rags."

"You're quite correct," he agreed, "I have no idea, and the results are certainly not worth a moment's discomfort. I assume you got quite a quizzing after you went upstairs last night." His sympathetic tones and their shared laughter did much to restore her normal good humor.

"Yes. Mama came to my room, and this is the result." She touched a ringlet with her fingers. "And I would hazard a guess that you won a lot of money from Lord Barrow, judging by his gloomy aspect at breakfast."

"He's a gamester, I'm afraid, Lady Emmeline. And I much fear that he'll soon start going through your mother's inheritance, if he hasn't started already." His grave countenance brought a responsive seriousness to Emmeline's face.

She looked worried and shook her head. "We don't live the way we did before mother married him. There are fewer servants, and less money to spend on gowns and other fripperies." She stopped suddenly, a hand to her mouth. "Oh dear. What was I thinking of? I'm sorry, my lord. I had no right to mention such things to you."

"It is forgotten," he assured her. "You have my word that it will go no further."

They had reached the stables and Jack came out to greet them.

"No ridin' for ye today, milady, by the looks o' it," he said with a familiar grin.

"No, Jack, not today. I've just brought Lord Charles to see Thunder and Lovely Lady, and I'm hoping that he'll show me that matched pair of grays he's driving."

Jack nodded. "Pair o' beauties an' no mistake, milady. Cost 'is lordship a pretty penny I'll be bound."

Completely comfortable in the company of stableboys and grooms, who held her in affectionate respect, she seemed like a different person, her face glowing happily. She made a delightful picture as she discussed with animation the merits of each animal. Charles could not fail to notice the change, and wondered how this lovely girl had retained her natural charm in such a household.

The stable was one area where Lord Barrow had not yet started to cut back. They spent the better part of an hour there, and it was with reluctance that they returned to the house. Once there, however, Charles suddenly realized he needed to talk further with Jack regarding his grays, and as Lady Barrow approached them, he excused himself to return to the stables.

It took but a moment to explain to Jack the special handling his cattle required before their departure, and he was about to return to the house when the groom cleared his throat noisily to get his attention, then motioned with his head toward a small office by the side of the stables. Curious, Charles went inside, and Jack followed a moment later.

"Growin' into a real beauty, Lady Emmeline is, milord . . ." he started with some hesitation and shaking of his head. "Not my place, sir, an' I knows it, but there's nobody else to say owt . . . T'new lord whips 'er somethin' cruel, an' fer little or nothin'. Jack, she says t'me one day, I've got to get away soon, I can't stand it any longer. Can't take much more, poor mite, an' 'er mother does nowt about it."

The old man looked very worried. "Told me, i' confidence o' course, she did, but she's thinkin o' runnin' off to London to find a job wi' a good family. Per'aps yer lordship might know some such family where she'd be 'appy. Dursen't let new lord know, tho', or e'd beat 'er 'alf t'death."

Charles had suspected something of the sort because of the incident at dinner the night before. He was very sorry for the girl, but did not see what he could do to help. However, he did not wish to appear unfeeling. There was a remote chance his sister could use some help, though he wouldn't wish her brats on anyone.

"It will go no further, Jack, have no fear of that. I'll give it some thought—see if anything can be done for her." With what he hoped was a reassuring smile, and a pat on the back, he bade the old man a good day and returned to the house.

AFTER A LIGHT LUNCHEON Charles's curricle was brought around and he said his farewells. Lord and Lady Barrow were insistent in their invitation to him to stop by on his return, but he made no commitment and implied that he would return directly from the Grahams' to his parents' home.

As soon as the small vehicle was out of sight, Emmeline turned to go indoors, but was stopped short by the voice of her stepfather.

"Just where do you think you're going, Emmeline?" he demanded sternly, and waited for her reply.

"I was going to see if there was anything I could do to help Agatha, sir. She's starting a new piece of needlework and—"

"Oh no, missy, you stay right here. Your mother and I have something to say to you." His expression was ugly. "I gave my word, and I'll not punish you for your behavior yesterday afternoon, but you'll not do it again. The maids have burned all those breeches you were so fond of wearing, and in future you'll ride sidesaddle like a lady." He paused to let his words sink in. "As soon as I find a buyer, that colt, Thunder, will be sold, and you will use a more suitable mount."

"No, please don't sell him," Emmeline begged, not daring to move closer to her stepfather but pleading with her hands. "I promise I'll never ride him again if only you'll keep him here."

A satisfied smile twisted the cruel mouth of Lord Barrow. "You heard what I said. He'll fetch a pretty good price in a private sale."

Close to tears, she turned to her mother who for once showed some compassion. Taking Emmeline's hand, she led her indoors. "Come along. Let's see what Agatha's doing with her embroidery."

Three

The shooting at the Grahams' was everything an avid sportsman could have wished, and Lord Charles Carruthers even had the good fortune to hook some fair-sized trout in the nearby streams, but after less than a sennight he grew weary of the masculine company and kept recalling a pair of sapphire-blue eyes more frequently than he would have believed possible.

He reminded himself of the many far more beautiful young ladies of his acquaintance, who were poised, and knew how to say the right things or say nothing at all when the occasion demanded. She'd not yet made her come-out and the way things stood with Lord Barrow, it seemed likely she never would. He might release enough funds for the older girl to have a Season, her marriage to some wealthy older man being an investment, but it would seem he had more than a disaffection for Lady Emmeline and was not likely to raise a finger to help her.

Charles frowned as he remembered Lord Barrow's unsavory reputation. What if Barrow was just waiting for an opportunity to have the girl himself, as well as having the mother? The head groom had implied Barrow almost appeared to take pleasure in punishing her. Suppose he should wish to hurt her in other ways? His eyes darkened at that possibility and it took considerable effort to control his revulsion. The idea of that middle-aged roué touching the soft, white skin of the little one was not to be conceived.

In his mind's eye he saw her riding her colt, her blond tresses tied back, but wisps still flying behind her, leaning over the young horse's neck, and though he couldn't hear her, he was sure she was talking softly to the colt, coaxing him to go faster and faster like the wind.

There was no virtue in delay. It would take but two hours, and he could be with her for a little while. He'd have to go slowly at first—she was young for her age and so innocent.

He suddenly sprang to his feet. What kind of crass-brained notion had entered his head? She was a nice child, refreshingly honest, but that was all! She expected nothing from him—it was her parents who had ambitions, and her groom who was worried about her.

But then there was that laugh. He smiled at the thought. When she was free of the others for a while, she had laughed as ladies never do, putting all her heart in it. A joy to see and hear, and quite irresistible. But if she remained in that house much longer, they'd break her spirit. Something must be done!

THE GRAHAMS WERE hard-pressed to understand why, after coming all this way, he chose to leave so soon. They tried to cajole him into staying, but he was adamant.

He gave his valet instructions to pack, and sent him on ahead, this time to his parents' home. Then, traveling as light as possible, he turned his grays once more in the direction of Grantley Range.

EMMELINE SAT GAZING out of the window of her bedchamber. Until her father's death two years ago, almost everything she could see from this window had been theirs. But the estate and title had passed to a distant cousin. Fortunately, the cousin already had more houses than he needed, and had agreed that the widow should stay on at Grantley Range for the rest of her life, while he put a steward in to manage the estate.

At first there had been ample wherewithal for their needs, as her father had a considerable inheritance on his mother's side. He had once told her there was sufficient to take care of them, give each girl a Season in London, and provide each with a ten-thousand-pound dowry. However, shortly before her remarriage her mother had said that Lord Grantley's money had all been left in her keeping and would be placed in Lord Barrow's charge as soon as they were wed.

Lord Barrow had started to call at the house not quite a year after her father's death, and he had, of course, been equally charming to all three daughters. He was a number of years older than Lady Grantley, but had retained a slim figure, and his suave good looks were most appealing to a widow just getting over her loss and feeling the need of a man's care.

She had always been a very self-centered woman, caring more for herself, her jewelry and clothes than for her husband and three daughters, particularly Emmeline, who was so very different from herself and the other girls.

Flattered when Lord Barrow showed his interest so soon after the death of Lord Grantley, she saw marriage to him as a chance to resume the social life she had enjoyed so much as a young girl. He seemed to spend most of his time in London, knew many of the *ton* who had been her girlhood friends, and promised her the things she missed, such as Seasons in London each year as they brought out the three girls.

Lord Grantley had preferred a quiet country life, and she had never been able to persuade him to take her on his brief, infrequent business visits to that city. And just when the time neared when they would have to enter the social whirl once more to marry off their daughters, he had died and forced her to delay her plans and even spend a dreary year in black—never her best color.

But after Lord Barrow married her, he was shocked to find the family no longer owned Grantley Range and the surrounding estates as he had assumed, and it was then that his true character showed through.

Lady Barrow preferred not to notice his heavy drinking and gambling, and the numerous small economies he insisted they make in their way of life. He convinced her that it was of the utmost importance for him to be well dressed in order to bring off the deals that he was making on his frequent trips alone to London.

He played up to her avarice by promising her a London townhouse and all the servants, jewelry, and fine clothes she could wish if she would be patient for a little while longer and help him without question, when needed, to achieve his aims. She had readily agreed, and at his suggestion had enlisted the aid of Agatha, who was particularly good at entertaining the friends he brought to stay overnight.

One day when Lord Barrow as away, Emmeline had looked through some of the family accounts in the study, and had found them most revealing until her mother had walked in and caught her. Emmeline pretended to be looking for something else, but knew she was not believed, and it was soon after this that the vicious streak in her mother's nature had been vented on her. Lord Barrow had been informed and he had punished her by forbidding many of the things her father had allowed. From then on, he had dealt with her transgressions swiftly and painfully, with her mother's complete approval.

Just two days ago, he had sold her colt, Thunder, to a "gentleman farmer" who lived some twenty miles to the north, and Jack had told her that he was also planning the sale of her filly, Lovely Lady.

Agatha had not spoken to her since the night when she had stormed into her bedroom, her mother alternated between extreme criticism and cool disapproval, and even Charlotte had started to take her cues from the attitude of the others.

The appetite her mother and sisters had despised in her as unladylike had now disappeared, and she had spent most of the last two days sitting listlessly in her bedchamber, not wishing to mount sidesaddle one of the horses designated by her stepfather. Her last real freedom had been on Thunder the day Lord Charles had arrived, she thought. She sighed, regretfully. He had been kinder to her than anyone had in the last two years, and she had dreamed of getting to know him better. Just the thought brought a flush to her pale cheeks. But it was too late now. He'd given every indication that he would not return, and she really couldn't blame him. She'd have to rely on herself to get away from the Range.

At Lord Grantley's insistence, Emmeline had received an excellent education for a girl. Under the tutelage of a proficient governess, Miss Cuttle, and the curate in the village, she had studied French and Latin, geography and history in addition to piano and voice, painting and drawing, and several forms of needlework. She could add, subtract, divide, and multiply, and had a sound knowledge of English language, literature, and poetry. Her governess had likened her to a sponge that absorbs readily, and this stood her in good stead, for she now felt qualified to obtain a position as governess.

Quite uninformed about such matters, she thought it would be easy to get a position with some family, as had

Miss Cuttle, and spend her days teaching bright little children to read and write, playing with them, loving them and being loved and needed in turn. She would soon have enough money to pay for an inside seat on the stage to London and lodging for a short stay while she made an application for a post. Although no one but Jack knew it, her father had given her bright shillings and florins each time she jumped a higher hurdle or ran a faster race. She had kept them hidden away, and added to them with small economies in her meager allowance for gloves stockings and such.

Also hidden away was the address in London of a respectable boarding house where Miss Cuttle had stayed after she had left their employ, and Emmeline planned to take lodging there immediately she reached London.

Her need to leave home was becoming increasingly acute as Lord and Lady Barrow became more spiteful toward her. And there was something else that she couldn't talk to anyone about, particularly her mother. It was the feeling that Lord Barrow's interest in her was not quite fatherly. She tried not to get too close to him, as he was always touching her in a way that he didn't touch her sisters, and she was even more afraid of that than of his beatings.

Therefore, it was essential that he never find her after she left. In the meantime, she would behave as normally as possible, and once she made her escape, she would have to get right away so she would not be found and brought back.

An unexpected knock on her door interrupted her thoughts. It was only a little past luncheon, which she rarely ate when in the house, and it was some time yet before the dinner hour. The maid who answered her call to enter brought a message from her mother that she had a visitor and was to join them in the drawing room looking her best.

"Who is it, Annie? Did you see?" she asked, not really expecting to be told, as she was one of the maids her stepfather had hired, and the one who had searched for and burned her breeches.

"No, milady. I didn't see anyone," the maid answered pertly with a toss of her head.

The dress she was wearing was really not very creased, so she smoothed the faded sprigged muslin with her hands, and then rebraided her hair.

She knew it had to be a man when she heard the high, tinkling pitch of her mother's voice through the drawing room door—it was the voice her mother always used when talking to men. When she entered the room, however, she was unprepared to see Lord Charles Carruthers. He turned as the door opened and her heart skipped a beat at the sight of his warm, understanding smile.

Recovering from her surprise, she dropped a curtsy, and he came toward her, taking her hand in his.

"I wonder, Lady Barrow, if I might take your daughter for a stroll in the garden?" He asked permission, but would have been astounded had he received anything other than an affirmative answer.

Once outside, Charles and Emmeline walked in silence until they reached the rose garden, where a seat was conveniently located under a bower of climbing pink blossoms. When he had made sure she was comfortable, he turned a concerned eye on her. "Have you been ill, Lady Emmeline? You don't appear as well as when I left some seven days ago," he said, his voice kind and soothing.

"He—my stepfather sold Thunder, and he's going to sell Lovely Lady," she blurted out, with such anguish in her voice he found it hard to believe anyone would want to hurt her so.

"Was it because you rode him again wearing breeches?"

he asked soothingly, trying to find a reason why her horses and not some others would be sold.

She shook her head. "I didn't. They had taken my breeches and burned them while I showed you the stables. And your curricle was still in sight when he told me he would sell the horses. It seems I did not please you as I should have," she said sadly.

"But you pleased me very much indeed, Lady Emmeline." The perfect answer to both her problem and his own came to him swiftly, as though it had been hovering in his head, just waiting for the right moment to surface. "So much, in fact, that I have returned to ask for your hand in marriage. I know I should first speak with your stepfather, but I would not wish him to push you into something for which you might have a dislike."

Once the words were out, he felt a simple, profound relief. This was the reason he had been so uncommonly glad to get away from the hospitality of the Grahams. Now all he had to do was convince her, as she was looking far from delighted by the prospect. He thought of the prompt response he would have received from the many young ladies he had known in his rakish past, and smiled ruefully.

He reached once more for her hand, and placed it in his own large one, the warmth of his touch giving her a feeling more exciting than that of just comfort and protection.

"But you don't love me." It was a statement, not a question, and she looked directly at him, her blue eyes seeming larger because of the sooty lashes fringing them.

"No, not yet," he admitted, "and you don't love me, but I believe we could deal very satisfactorily with each other, and in time love might grow, as so often is the case. I believe also that you have a need to get away from here." He was trying hard to rationalize his feelings.

Now that he was with her once more, he felt a tremendous urge to protect her, and not allow anyone to hurt her again or destroy her charming innocence.

"No matter what I say, I know my stepfather will agree. He's been anxious for one of us to make a good marriage," she said quietly. "You'd best ask about a dowry. My father told me he was leaving ten thousand pounds for each of us."

"Very well, I will find out, although it is of little consequence as I am a man of considerable wealth and prospects. Is there anything you would like to know about me?" he asked.

She shook her head, and he realized that she had not smiled even faintly during the whole conversation. He touched the velvety softness of her cheek with one gentle finger, feeling the warm flush that spread beneath it.

"If you have no wish to wed, you may decline my offer, you know." His tone was soft and infinitely patient. "And you need have no fear, no one will ever know I asked you."

She saw his brows arched in question as she looked deeply into his kind eyes. "If I must marry—and there's little doubt of it—then I would very much like it to be to you," she breathed softly.

His roving finger now delicately traced the outline of her lips, and she felt them strangely swollen by his featherlight touch.

With a rueful smile he said gruffly, "Very well. I suppose I must be satisfied with that answer." Then he stood. Leaving her in the rose garden, he went in search of her stepfather.

Emmeline didn't move, but stayed on the bench until shadows began to gather. She had never thought of marriage as a means of getting away from home, but it was as good a way as any, she realized. That was, of course, provided Lord Charles continued to be kind to her. He was the first man, other than her father, with whom she'd felt any closeness, and it surprised her to find that his lightest touch made her feel excited, as though her heart beat faster, and her breathing quickened.

But he might change once they were married. Lord Barrow had stopped being nice to them immediately after the wedding, and if this should happen again with Lord Charles, she determined that she would not remain and spend more unhappy years, but would run away and find work rather than stay with a tyrant.

Then there was his family. Suppose they didn't like her, perhaps wanted their son to marry a sophisticated young lady instead of a little country mouse? She should have asked him questions about them when she had the opportunity.

Before she left the bower, she reached up and plucked a rosebud to take to her bedchamber.

She changed once more into the white satin gown, it being the only one she possessed that was even slightly in vogue, and once again she braided her hair into coils at the back of her neck. She saw in the mirror the reason for his question about her health, as her eyes were ringed with shadows now, and her oval face looked pinched.

The maid came to her door with the message that she was to go directly to the drawing room, and she thanked her quietly but took a little longer than needed before obeying the instruction. She'd made her decision and she knew what would await her downstairs.

Lord Barrow looked as though he had already started to celebrate, as an opened bottle of champagne stood on a small table.

"Come in, Emmeline. We have cause for celebration," he said, his greedy eyes gleaming with pleasure. "Lord Charles has formally asked for your hand in marriage, and I have been pleased to accept on your behalf."

"Without asking me, of course, my lord," she said mildly.

"Of course I didn't ask you," he responded irritably. "How can you know what is best for you? You will do as you're told, and like it."

Finally she smiled, a ghost of her former smile, without a trace of a dimple. "As I accepted his lordship's offer this afternoon before you returned home, your agreement was simply confirmation of my decision, sir."

"You are impertinent, girl," he started, with a snarl of rage, but remembered himself as Charles moved to Emmeline's side and placed a protective arm around her waist. The butler handed her a glass of champagne, and she allowed them to toast her health, while she took only a sip of the heady beverage, then put it aside, feeling the bubbles pricking her nose.

This time Charles was seated by her side at dinner, and he watched as she merely nibbled the food. He kept offering her some of the various dishes of salmon, turkey, and ham, and she took a little to please him, but then just pushed it around the plate, finding it almost impossible to swallow anything.

When they finished the main course, Lord Barrow stood up to make a speech about losing a daughter, and the slight appetite she had left disappeared entirely.

"I would like the wedding to be as soon as possible, within two weeks if you could be ready in time, Lady Emmeline," Charles informed her. "My father is in poor health, and it would be best not to prolong the engagement under the circumstances. I will send an announcement to the *Gazette* tomorrow. Regrettably, none of my family will be present. My mother would not, of course, leave my father alone, and my only sibling is expecting her fourth child within a few months."

She realized he had initially taken for granted her acceptance of his proposal and now her agreement to an early wedding date. But she didn't protest; she too was anxious to get the wedding over with. She wished he could love her now, even just a little, but he'd said it could grow, and the sooner they were married, the sooner it might start.

THE NEXT TWO WEEKS were very busy as Lady Barrow, at Lord Charles's request and his expense, tried to fit her daughter out with a small, fashionable wardrobe. It had been decided that she would be wed in a very simple ivory-colored gown that would make an attractive ball gown later, instead of wasting money on an elaborate bride's dress that couldn't be worn again.

Emmeline did not argue about anything. She was not at all interested in the trappings that went with a wedding, and allowed the others to decide what style suited her and what colors and fabrics should be used. She was aware that a number of gowns were also being ordered for Agatha and her mother, and added to the bill, but made no comment as it kept them in better humor toward her.

Charles had left for his parents home the very next day after they became engaged. Every morning before any of the family arose, Emmeline crept downstairs and out to the seat in the rose bower. After sitting for a few minutes, inhaling the delicate fragrance and remembering his touch and his gentle proposal, she would pick another rosebud and take it back to her bedchamber to dream about the new warmth and awareness that had entered her life, that her stepfather couldn't take away. But, just to be sure, she wouldn't tell anyone how she felt, not even Jack. She just wished the days would pass more swiftly until Charles returned and their vows were exchanged.

The evening before he came back, Lady Barrow accompanied Emmeline to her bedchamber as she was about to retire for the night. She closed the door behind her and as she came into the room, her glance fell on the rosebud Emmeline had picked that morning.

"I think it's time we had a nice little coze, my girl," she began. "We have never discussed a wife's duties, as I felt there was time enough after Agatha married."

Emmeline looked questioningly at her mother, who had rarely attempted to discuss anything with her before other than her unladylike behavior.

Her mother's eyes went sardonically to the rosebud and then back to Emmeline. "Very sweet. I suppose he gave you one when he proposed." Emmeline's cheeks flushed with embarrassment. "Don't be self-conscious, my dear. This is the romantic period in your relationship. Every girl goes through it, and it would be well to make the most of it now, for there's seldom much romance after the wedding, and particularly when it's an arranged marriage such as this one."

"Arranged, Mama? I don't understand."

Her mother nodded. "The marriage was arranged by your father and his, and put in writing when you were a babe of three years. But, of course, the old marquess had no intention of honoring the agreement until I called it to his attention."

"But why me? Why not Agatha?" Emmeline asked, a cold, unwanted feeling creeping over her.

"I don't rightly know, Emmeline. Frankly, I can't imagine why anyone would choose you over Agatha. Your father didn't say which daughter, and I suppose Lord Charles felt you'd be the easier to control and mold to his ways. And he will control you, my girl, and turn you into a more obedient wife than you've been a daughter. Once those vows have been exchanged, he owns you for the rest of your life, you cannot refuse him anything."

She waited, spitefully, for the effect of her words to sink in.

"He'll be wanting an heir as fast as possible, and I've no doubt he'll bed you nightly until he's sure one's on the way."

"Bed me?" Emmeline asked, having no idea what her mother was talking about.

"You must know, girl. You've been around animals all your life. But just you remember you're not an animal, and must behave like a lady. You must close your eyes and think of something pleasant. I always think of choosing a new gown, picking out the materials and the trims, and trying it on in front of a mirror. Do that, and it'll soon be over and he'll be back in his own bed."

Emmeline's face was closed and expressionless. "Is it very painful, Mama?"

"Quite painful at first, and always very distasteful. You won't enjoy it, but ladies are not supposed to enjoy it. Men of rank have Cyprians, women they keep for their pleasure that way. And I've no doubt Lord Charles already has some such arrangement.

"For all his lazy drawl, he's a powerful-looking young man, and I'd advise you to behave yourself right from the start. A beating from him would be much more painful than the ones Lord Barrow gives you."

"But he's not like that," Emmeline protested. "He's always been very gentle and kind."

"One of your troubles, Emmeline, is that you don't mind me when I'm speaking to you," her mother snapped irritably. "I told you that men are one way before marriage, and completely different the moment the ring is on your finger. 'Twas a lucky thing I was on good terms with the doctor, else your father would have gone on trying for a boy forever. As it was, it cost me a deal of money to get that doctor to tell him I mustn't have any more children or I would lose my life."

Lady Barrow bent and placed a cold kiss on Emmeline's cheek, then flounced out of the chamber, sure in her own mind that she'd done her duty by her daughter, and prepared her adequately for marriage, as she'd promised Lord Charles.

Emmeline had endured the monologue in silence, but once she was alone she became quite distraught as she remembered her mother's words. She asked herself if she had been wise in accepting his lordship's offer so quickly. Could she be committing herself to an even worse situation than the one she had here at the Range?

CHARLES RETURNED the day before the wedding, surprising Emmeline as she returned from a walk in the woods.

"What an unexpected pleasure, my dear," he said, as he dismounted to walk his horse alongside of her. "And I believe you're looking much more yourself."

Flustered at the unexpected meeting, she blushed and said shyly, "Thank you, my lord. I do feel better."

"I've brought something for you, which I'd much rather give you out here than in front of the family." His eyes were teasing as he reached into a pocket of his voluminous riding coat and took out something which he held away from her. "You only get it if you promise to start calling me Charles."

Emmeline loved surprise presents and until last night would have shown her delight, but now a coolness was apparent as she glanced at the small package in his hand. "I promise to try—Charles," she agreed quietly.

She tore off the wrapping, opened the box, and her eyes widened in surprise, then brimmed with tears.

"It's too beautiful for me, my—Charles," she said breathlessly.

Taking her arm, he walked over to some trees and secured his horse. Then he turned her toward him, but she dropped her head to stop him seeing her tears. Gently, he cradled her face in his hands and tilted it upward. "It matches your beautiful eyes, little one," he said softly, taking the box from her hand and slipping the sapphire ring onto her finger. "And I like the way you say my—Charles." He touched her forehead with his lips before taking out a handkerchief and wiping her eyes.

They walked back to the house and parted in the hall, promising to meet at dinner, and Emmeline hurried to her bedchamber, needing to be alone with her conflicting emotions. She fingered the ring, which fit her finger perfectly, and was the most beautiful jewel she had ever seen.

As she turned it around and around, watching the brilliant color flash from the stone, she came back to reality, out of the fearful state she'd been in ever since her mother's little coze. Unable to find her usual outlet in riding, since riding sidesaddle was more of a frustration than a release, she had taken a long walk across the estate, but even this had not given her peace of mind.

She was betrothed to a stranger and was giving herself to him tomorrow. Suppose her mother was right and he did stop being kind to her? What if he did keep a mistress? He'd asked her if she had any questions, and now it was too late to ask them. But she had to get away from Grantley Range, at whatever cost, and this was a way.

THE WEDDING WAS as pleasant as any wedding could be when the bride went down the aisle on the arm of a man she hated, to marry a man she scarcely knew.

Emmeline had succumbed to a moment of panic again as she had dresed with the help of her mother's abigail in the simple ivory gown. Her hair had been piled high on the top of her head and a dozen or more white rosebuds entwined in it before the long veil had been pinned into place. It seemed as if everything was proceeding in an inevitable pattern and she was being swept along without the ability to stop it even had she so desired.

They said their vows, his loud and clear, and hers scarcely loud enough for even the first row of the congregation to hear.

Yesterday he had given her the beautiful sapphire ring, square cut and surrounded by diamonds, but the wedding band he slipped on her finger today was plain gold and very heavy, and she silently likened it to a ball and chain.

The service finally came to an end, and the bridegroom kissed the bride lightly on the forehead before tucking her hand in his arm and walking down the aisle and into the carriage to return to the Range, where a light meal had been arranged on two sideboards in the dining room. She ate little, despite the fact that it would be a long time before she was able to eat again. There were endless toasts, which she was sure Charles hated as much as she did for the falseness of most. Lord Barrow's gambling and other passions had not served to make him very popular in the countryside.

The wedding cake was cut at last, and she was able to return to her old bedchamber to change into a carriage dress of sturdy light beige bombazine trimmed with chocolate brown. Her matching beige bonnet was also trimmed in brown and lined with cream silk, and beige kid gloves and short boots completed the ensemble. A glance in the mirror told her she was no longer the young tomboy who was such a misfit in the family, but in just a few hours she had been transformed into an elegant young matron.

While Charles, at his own instigation, had an interview with Lord Barrow in the study, Emmeline paid a farewell visit to the stables, not to see her favorite horses, as these were already gone, but to stay goodbye to Jack. He had been such a good friend, but now he stood back in awe at her transformation, and she had to almost fling herself into his arms for the warm hug she needed from him.

"Just ye make 'im a good wife, milady, like yer father would've wanted. 'E's a fine man and'll take good care of ye, I know." His voice broke a little, and he pushed her away roughly before she saw the tears in his old eyes.

Charles's carriage, which had arrived late yesterday, was large enough to accommodate her few small trunks and in the early afternoon they started out on the long journey south to his own country seat in Warwickshire, which he had inherited from a bachelor uncle.

Four

For much of the journey Emmeline was alone in the carriage, as her bridegroom much preferred to ride alongside, joining her for only short intervals, and even then seeming to have little to say. She tried to prolong the periods of companionship by showing some interest in her future surroundings. When asked to describe the home to which he was taking her, however, he said there was no point when she would see it for herself in such a short while. And when she ventured to inquire about his parents he was rather curt with her, explaining that he planned to take her to see them within a week of their return, as they were most anxious to meet her.

What he did not tell her was that although his father had been in reasonably fair health when he had last seen him, some six days before, he had a strange feeling, almost a foreboding about the marquess and was anxious to get home as quickly as possible in case there should be a message waiting. Had he been alone, he could have covered the distance in half the time. Subconsciously he was blaming Emmeline for the slow pace of the carriage.

He did describe the antics of his sister's children in some detail, and she smilingly commented that they were being lovingly spoiled and would be in for a terrible time when they were sent away to school. But there the conversation ended and Charles mounted his horse, leaving Emmeline alone in the carriage once more, with only her doubts and misgivings about marriage that her mother had deliberately implanted in her mind.

So far there had been nothing to persuade her that her mother was wrong, for the thoughtfulness and kindness Lord Charles had shown prior to the wedding had since been markedly absent. His reticence even when they stopped for the night was particularly disquieting, and although she was relieved when he bespoke separate bedchambers for them, she was rapidly working herself into a state of despair at the mistake she had so obviously made. It would have been far better, she thought, to have declined his proposal and waited until she had saved sufficient funds to strike out on her own.

To a young girl who had never made a journey of more than three or four hours, this one seemed endless, and she felt the utmost relief when she saw they had turned onto a private road, and around a bend a large house came into view. A few weeks ago she would not have felt so tired, but the series of events which had occurred since she met Charles, with her resultant loss of appetite, had depleted her energy, and though it was the middle of the afternoon, she wished for nothing more than to find a comfortable bed and sleep for several hours.

But she was not to be granted her wish immediately, for on entering the hall they found all the servants had been assembled to meet their new mistress. The butler, an elderly man who stood very erect and aloof from the rest of the staff, obviously ruled over them with a rod of iron. Emmeline memorized his name, Jenkins, but as to the remainder of them, other than the housekeeper, Mrs. Carter, she could remember neither their names nor their faces.

Mrs. Carter gave her a quick tour of the ground floor of the house which, to her tired eyes, seemed much like any other, and then showed her to her bedchamber. Frightened of some strange person walking in, she turned the key in the lock after the housekeeper had gone. Her first impression was of a huge bed dominating the room, and then she saw a small chaise near the fireplace and sat there while removing her hat and gloves. She must have fallen asleep, for she awoke to a knocking on the door and, feeling decidedly bewildered in the strange surroundings, realized she was still fully dressed.

After a second knock, Charles entered through another door which she hadn't noticed earlier.

"Emmeline, why did you lock the door? The maid became worried when she couldn't get into the room. It has never been our family's custom to lock doors and I trust you will not do so again." In her confused state, he sounded quite severe, and she couldn't understand what all the fuss was about. Dropping asleep like that had been a mistake as now her weariness was aggravated by a throbbing headache.

"Well, my family has always locked doors," she said quite emphatically, "and if I don't wish to be disturbed, then I shall turn the key. That's what it's for, isn't it?"

He moved swiftly across the room and, unlocking the door, pocketed the key. "Thus concludes our first argument." He spoke softly, but his brow was creased in a frown. "The journey was wearisome, my dear, I admit. I'll ask Mrs. Carter to send up the most promising maid to help you bathe and dress, and then, while we're at dinner, she can unpack your things."

"My lord . . ." she began, in an attempt to explain.

"My name is Charles, as you very well know. You'll

have to start getting used to it sometime, Emmeline." He was quite brusque with her now, as he'd asked her to use his first name many times during the long journey.

"Charles," she said, emphasizing his name, "why did you agree to marry me? I know it was arranged, but you could have had Agatha instead."

He looked thoughtfully at her. "Isn't it a little late to ask that question?" One eyebrow was raised rather rakishly. "For that matter, why did you marry me? I mean, besides wanting to get away from that dreadful house?"

She was still very tired, and his attitude regarding the key made her sure that her mother had the right of it. He had changed. He was different now that the ring was on her finger. She felt an instinct to fight back.

"There was no other reason," she told him coldly. "If it hadn't been you, it would have been the next man who offered—or, when I had managed to save up enough money, I'd have run off and set out on my own."

He laughed derisively. "Have you any idea what might have happened to you if you'd left home on your own? Where on earth did you think you would go?"

"I'd have gone to London and gotten a position, of course. I have been very well educated, and I could easily become a governess," she told him proudly.

"Oh, Emmeline." He started to laugh. "You little innocent— "

This was too much. "Don't you dare laugh at me, you . . . you . . ." Her eyes flashed, and before he realized her intention she had slapped him across his left cheek.

She'd never hit anyone before, and had no idea what would happen next, but she was not long in finding out. With one hand, he caught her wrist in a bone-crunching grip while with his other hand he grabbed her chin and fiercely yanked it up so that she was looking up into his blazing eyes.

He towered over her, glaring angrily. "You want to know why I married you, do you? Well, I'll tell you. I married you because I have to produce an heir, and you'd better be a virgin and very fertile if you want to keep me happy," he roared, releasing her so suddenly that she fell back against the chaise. His voice still rang in her ears as she heard the door slam.

All the agonies of the past came flooding back to her—the loss of her beloved horses, her stepfather's hate, the taunts of her mother and sisters, the wedding, the exhausting journey—and her chin hurt terribly.

During their brief courtship, he had appeared to be so gentle and kind, admitting honestly that he didn't love her but giving her hope that there was some affection there that would grow with the years. She had trusted him, as he reminded her very much of her father and gave her reason to wish for the first time for a happy life with a good husband and children of her own.

How could he, she asked herself, have been so cruel as to make her travel all the way alone and then, when she was so tired she was hardly responsible for her actions, treat her so viciously? Hiding her head in the pillow, she sobbed as though her heart would break in this strange room, strange house, strange part of the country, and with this stranger for a husband.

THE FIRELIGHT FLICKERING in the room was the only light, and night was descending when Emmeline finally stood up, dried her eyes, and tried to see what she looked like. She was lighting a candle on the dressing table when Charles entered the chamber again.

"I've just received a message from my mother. My

father is gravely ill, and I must leave right away," he told her.

Worry for the marquess was evident on his face. "You love them, don't you?" she said, thinking of her own father and understanding his distress.

He nodded. "Very much." He paused, obviously debating what he should do. "I can't take you with me, as a further long trip would be cruel in your present state of exhaustion, and I can travel faster alone. But in view of our earlier conversation, I'm concerned that you might try to run away. I'd like your solemn promise that you'll stay here. If you won't give it to me, I'll have no option but to lock you in your room until I return. Jenkins will have to be your jailer and bring up your meals."

Emmeline was outraged that he would think to treat her in such a way.

"How can you be certain that I might not overpower him and make off with the family jewels?" she asked, her eyes flashing in anger. "Perhaps, if you could delay your journey a few moments, sir, Jenkins could search the cellars for a ball and chain."

He eyed her coldly. "You can come down out of the boughs, Emmeline. I have expressed my distaste at using such extreme measures, but your attitude leaves me no alternative."

"My attitude, my lord? If I recall correctly, it was your completely unreasonable attitude regarding my use of the key to my chamber that started this quite ridiculous brangle. But it served one most useful purpose. You were finally honest about your reasons for marrying me, and I at least now know where I stand in your eyes." She gulped helplessly as tears threatened.

Ignoring her outburst, he said calmly, "I am awaiting your commitment."

There was a long pause. He had given her something

to consider. She hadn't seriously thought of running away until he put the idea into her head. Perhaps it might be the best thing to do.

"I'll promise," she said finally, with a deep sigh, her crossed fingers hidden in the folds of her dress.

He put out a hand and drew her toward him, looking carefully at her tearstained face, bruised chin, and obvious signs of complete weariness. His fingers lightly stroked her face, surprisingly soothing and comforting. "When I return we must both try to deal better with each other."

Emmeline made no answer, but looked at him gravely.

"I've ordered a bath to be brought to you in ten minutes, and supper here in your room half an hour later. Then I think you'll be ready for a good night's rest. Don't forget your promise, and if I'm not able to get back in a few days, I'll send you word."

He touched his lips briefly to her forehead, then he was gone, and a few minutes later his orders were carried out. As soon as the footmen had brought up the copper tub and jugs of hot water, a little maid by the name of Jeannie helped her undress, but then Emmeline dismissed her as she was accustomed to bathing herself, and had solved many a problem while soaking in a hot bath.

The tension eased in her tired body as the warm, perfumed bubbles drew the weariness out of her, and after she'd soaped herself thoroughly she slid down into the comforting water until only her head was visible. Now she could think more clearly.

It would appear, she decided, that everything he'd done since putting the heavy ring on her finger confirmed her mama's predictions. He had shown no enjoyment whatever in her company, although she had to admit to herself that she'd been far more comfortable alone in the carriage. He had dominated her, threatened her, and bullied her, she told herself, deliberately disregarding the fact that she hit him first, and had not treated him with the respect that was his due.

Why not carry out her original plan and go to London to seek employment? Then he could get an annulment and marry someone more to his liking. It was really a case of now or never, as once he returned there'd be no further opportunity. He had thought of it before she had, and so he would be watching her very carefully when he got back.

She must make her escape before the servants arose at dawn, and that faithful butler started to watch her every movement on his master's behalf. Childishly, she felt she wasn't breaking her promise, for her fingers had been crossed when she had given it. At least she was a good deal closer to London, thanks to that endless carriage ride.

She ate as much supper as she could and then, before the tray was removed, took a scarf from a drawer and wrapped in it some meat, fresh fruit, and cheese that would not suffer too much by being transported.

By this time she was in need of rest, but dared not sleep too long as she must be away well before first light. She need not have worried about oversleeping, however, for her excitement acted like a charm and woke her at just the right time. She packed her plain, darker dresses into a small bag, together with underwear and nightwear, making sure that the bag did not weigh too much for her to carry, since she would probably have to walk many miles to the nearest posting house.

She carefully worded a brief note to Jenkins, making it seem that she was going to stay with friends in the neighborhood, saying that by prior arrangement these friends were to pick her up at seven in the morning, and that she had left to meet them, but expected to be back before Lord Charles returned. She left the note on her dressing table, in hopes that it would serve to account for her absence and prevent anyone looking for her right away.

She crept out of the house—just in time, for she could hear the servants starting to stir in the rooms above. As she had seen the long driveway only once and little more of the main highway, it was difficult to find her way, but when she stepped onto the main road she felt certain that she was heading in the right direction for the posting house.

After she was out of sight of the manor, she put down her bag and rested for a few minutes, eating the remains of last night's dinner before setting out in the half-light before sunup. She was still tired after the long journey from Yorkshire, and had not yet had a full night's sleep, but she was determined to put as much distance as possible between herself and the house before daylight.

But an hour into her journey, Emmeline was already beginning to feel her bag getting heavier and her legs becoming tired. She knew she'd have to sit down and rest for a few moments as soon as she rounded the next bend in the road. When she reached the spot, however, she saw a carriage in the distance, and decided to keep walking rather than allow its occupants to observe her sitting on the bank.

It soon became obvious, though, that the carriage was not moving, and as she came closer she could see a heavyset woman standing by the side of the road, leaning over another who was lying on the grass.

Emmeline's quiet approach had gone unnoticed until she inquired, "Has someone been injured? Perhaps I can be of assistance, ma'am?"

When the large woman turned around, it was obvious from her wrinkled face and gray hair that she was quite old. Her glance swept over Emmeline from head to toe, noting the plain but expensive cut of her dress and cloak, in keeping with the genteel voice.

"As you can see," she said, pointing to the vehicle, "we've lost a wheel from the carriage. You can't help there much, I'll guarantee. And Harriet here didn't have the good sense to hang on to the carriage, and went sailing right out of the door." Her black bonnet was slightly askew, and she was a little pale, but her words were uttered in a loud emphatic voice that matched her size.

Emmeline put down her bag and approached Harriet. She could see a rapidly swelling ankle, and the sobbing woman appeared to be in considerable discomfort. She was dressed in sober brown, and looked as though she might be a paid companion to the other.

"I can see her ankle is swollen . . ." Emmeline started to say when the heavy woman gave an angry snort.

"Anyone with a pair of eyes in their head can see that," she snapped. "And no doubt she's a few bruises because of her stupidity, but there's no call for her to blubber like a baby."

Harriet sniffed and blew her nose loudly.

"Tom's gone to fetch a doctor, if he can find one in the next town, and to hire another conveyance. But if he does it as well as he drives a coach, I'll bet a monkey we're in for a long wait." With an impatient grunt she took another look at Harriet, then turned back to Emmeline. "Don't just stand there gawking, girl. I'm Lady Poole and if you don't know the name then you're a stranger to these parts. If you mean to help, then take a look at Harriet's ankle."

Wondering whether she should drop her ladyship a curtsy first, then deciding against it, Emmeline bent over to examine Harriet's ankle. It was even more swollen than when she first had seen it, and she hesitated, wondering whether or not to recommend removing the boot before the doctor arrived. As it would have to come off anyway, and would be even more difficult to take off later, she reached into her bag for a pair of scissors.

At the sight of them, Harriet screamed and Lady Poole glared. "What's that you're doing?" she demanded, fixing Emmeline with a fierce stare.

"Nothing unless you agree, your ladyship. But I believe it would be easier to cut off her boot now than wait until her ankle is even more swollen." She couldn't completely hide the exasperation she felt at their helplessness.

Lady Poole grunted again. "Good thinking, girl," she allowed with a nod.

As she snipped carefully at the soft boot, Emmeline's resentment at being called "girl" grew, but she realized she couldn't disclose her real name. If Lady Poole was well known in the neighborhood, then she was bound to know Lord Charles.

Once the constricting boot had been removed, Harriet was a great deal more comfortable, and her sobs gave way to just an occasional sniff.

"Well, girl, what do you propose to do now? Just sit and look at the swelling all morning?" Lady Poole's booming voice broke into Emmeline's deliberations, and she made a quick decision.

"That's exactly what I mean to do, your ladyship, until I know whether a doctor will be coming." She looked calmly into Lady Poole's ungrateful face. "And, what is more, my name isn't girl, it's Catherine Withers."

"I was wondering when you'd get around to introducing yourself—Mrs. Withers," Lady Poole barked, having noticed the gold wedding band on Emmeline's left hand. "And what is your husband doing while you roam the highways in the early morning hours, without so much as a maid to accompany you?"

Emmeline flushed with embarrassment, but was determined to hold her own against this crotchety old lady.

"Just because I stopped to offer you assistance is no reason for me to tell you the story of my life," she said, in as firm and dignified a manner as she could muster under the circumstances. "I am prepared to wait and see if a doctor is coming. If he is not, then I intend to send your coachman to get water from the stream I can hear gurgling down there, and bind the ankle with wet cloths." She looked the old lady straight in the eye. "If you would prefer that I do none of these things, then I will bid you good day and continue on my way."

A deep chuckle rumbled in Lady Poole's chest and set her cheeks quivering. For the first time, she really looked at Emmeline. "I admire spunk, my dear, and you have it!" Her eyes twinkled, as she suddenly became interested in the pretty chit. "Stay, by all means, and make Harriet as comfortable as you can. In return, we'll give you a ride to wherever it is you are walking. How's that?"

Emmeline smiled, dimpling prettily. "That would be most acceptable, your ladyship," she murmured, realizing that this could be a lucky encounter after all.

It was not long before a carriage came into view. The old coachman had surprised his mistress by procuring a conveyance, but confirmed her fears that there was not a doctor for miles.

There was some objection from Harriet when she found her petticoat being torn into strips, but her ankle was soon strapped comfortably and Emmeline and the coachman managed to lift her into the carriage, though not without some difficulty as Lady Poole insisted on instructing them as to how it should be done.

When Harriet was settled comfortably and Tom was making her ladyship's carriage secure against vandals until the blacksmith arrived, Lady Poole turned to Emmeline.

"If it's the post house you're walking to, you'd have had a long walk, for it's many miles yet, Mrs. Withers. As I promised, if you wish we will take you there now, but Harriet is uncomfortable and I'd like to get her home as soon as possible." She had another idea in mind. "If you're not in too much of a hurry, my dear, why don't you accompany us to Poole House. We've about another ten miles to go. It'd be a comfort for me to have you close in case Harriet needs help on the journey. You could spend the night and rest up for a fresh start in the morning. What do you say?"

Emmeline thought about the long walk ahead of her. As Charles would be away for some time, and she'd left the note for Jenkins saying that she was visiting friends, no one would be looking for her for a few days.

"I'll be glad to accompany you, Lady Poole. And, as it is of little consequence whether I reach my destination one day or the next, I would appreciate the rest."

Once her bag had been stowed with the other luggage, Emmeline entered the carriage. The two older ladies started to snore almost immediately, leaving Emmeline to enjoy looking out at the strange countryside, so much softer than the harsh Yorkshire landscape to which she was accustomed.

After a while she too put her head into a corner of the carriage, closed her eyes, and fell into a deep sleep.

"Mrs. Catherine Withers, is it?" A gruff voice cut into her slumbers, and Emmeline opened her eyes to see Lady Poole wide awake once more, and looking at her questioningly.

"Yes, your ladyship," she replied, still quite sleepy.

"And do you still feel that you owe me no explanation

as to how you came to be walking along the highway at that hour, Mrs. Withers?" She looked at Emmeline with a certain wryness in her expression.

Sighing heavily, Emmeline said ruefully, "I don't think I owe it to you, Lady Poole, but I know you're not going to leave me alone until I tell you." She prefaced her confession with the remark, "I'm sure you won't believe me, but I was sharing a post chaise with two other ladies of my acquaintance, and asked to be set down close to my destination." She gave a self-deprecating shrug of her shoulders. "I foolishly gave the driver the wrong directions, and they were already out of sight before I realized I was miles from where I wanted to be."

Lady Poole gave her a disbelieving glare. "And that's the story you're going to stick to, I've no doubt?"

Emmeline tried her most disarming smile. "That's right, Lady Poole."

"And just where is Mr. Withers supposed to be, young lady?" her ladyship asked drily.

"He passed away more than a year ago," Emmeline said, trying to look sad.

Giving her a very dubious stare, Lady Poole closed her eyes once more and proceeded to doze, at times quite loudly, for the rest of the journey.

Five

As soon as they reached Poole House, footmen hurriedly came out to carry Harriet to her bedchamber, a doctor was sent for, and the housekeeper took charge. Lady Poole declared that she'd had all the excitement she could cope with for one day, and promptly retired to her bedchamber.

It was an attractive house built in the Georgian style in red brick with white stone cornices and white painted trim. It looked as solid as its owner, but friendlier, and it gave Emmeline the feeling of being safe and secure.

The bedchamber to which she was shown was a pleasant room, if a little small and at the back of the house. A very young maid was assigned to her, but the girl was most eager to please, and Emmeline, who was by now very hungry, asked if she might first have tea and a small sandwich.

While she was waiting, she unpacked the items she would need for one night, assuming correctly that her ladyship would not be down for dinner and that hers would be served in her bedchamber.

As soon as her hunger was appeased and the dust of the road washed away, Emmeline stretched out on the bed. Exhausted still from her journey south and lack of sleep the previous night, she knew nothing further until a knock on the door heralded the little maid with a supper tray. Her appetite had returned, and she ate the light meal of crabmeat soup, poached salmon, and roasted chicken with much enthusiasm. Although unused to wine, she drank the whole glass which accompanied the meal, and even had a little of the syllabub. When the maid came to remove the tray, Emmeline inquired of her if the doctor had called on Miss Harriet, and was told that he had, and that she was resting comfortably, the ankle being sprained, not broken.

Had she not been a stranger in the house, Emmeline would have ventured down to the library at this hour and selected a book to pass the time before she once again felt sleepy, but not having been shown around the house, she had no idea in which direction the library might be, or indeed if one existed. So she prepared herself for the night and got into bed, piling the pillows behind her back, and then sat there thinking over the events of the last few days.

Inevitably her mind went directly to Charles, and she was surprised that she missed him. She began to wonder if he might, after all, be a good man despite the way he had treated her since the wedding. His haste to the side of his ailing father seemed to confirm this, and although it had hurt, she found she was no longer quite as angry with him for mistreating her. After all, she had started it.

He must have been beyond exhaustion by the time he reached his family home. Perhaps tonight he would get a good night's rest and find his father much better on the morrow. This was her hope for him.

What had he meant, she wondered, when he'd been so angry and talked about her being a virgin and fertile? She could only suppose it to have to do with having babies. Although she knew that male and female horses were put together and "mated" to produce a foal, Jack had always made sure that she didn't see what happened between them. This must be much the same as the bedding her mama had spoken of, and she was glad she'd escaped before that happened.

An early riser, she was up a few minutes before the maid came in to light the fire and bring water, and by the time the maid returned with a breakfast tray, Emmeline had repacked her bag and was ready to leave any time Lady Poole's carriage was ready.

She would, of course, have to see her ladyship before leaving, and she also wanted to see Harriet and find out how she was feeling.

She ate a hearty breakfast, but couldn't bring herself to put even a piece of bread into her scarf this time, as it somehow seemed like stealing.

After lingering in the bedchamber for more than half an hour, she thought the little maid had deserted her until she realized that she was probably waiting until she left before returning to collect the tray. With that thought, she made her way downstairs and into what appeared to be a morning room. She had hoped to see a footman of whom she could inquire, but the absence of any seemed evidence that everyone was usually abed at this hour, so she found a bell pull, gave it a tug, and waited.

Within a few minutes the startled housekeeper appeared.

"Why, Mrs. Withers, I thought you were still upstairs. What can I do for you?" she asked.

Emmeline appreciated the fact that she was probably very busy and came straight to the point. "As I am a stranger to this house and its occupants, I need to know at what hour I might see Lady Poole, and also if it is possible to visit Miss Harriet."

"Well, ma'am, both Lady Poole and Miss Harriet Jones, her ladyship's cousin, are having breakfast in their bedchambers. Lady Poole has expressed a wish to see you immediately after she is finished, and if you'd care to wait here, I'll have a maid come for you in a little while."

"Thank you, but if you could point me in the direction of the library, I'd prefer to wait there, if her ladyship wouldn't object." Emmeline smiled pleasantly, and was rewarded with an answering smile.

"If you'll come this way, ma'am."

In the library, she found a copy of Jane Austen's *Sense and Sensibility*, and settled down to reread some of the more interesting chapters until a maid arrived to take her to her mistress.

IF HER APPEARANCE was anything to judge by, it would seem that Lady Poole was not in any more amiable a mood than she had been on the highway the previous day. She was sitting up in bed with a wrap about her shoulders and a nightcap on her head, and she greeted Emmeline with a gruff, "Morning, ma'am—I collect you're averse to being called miss."

Emmeline dropped her a curtsy.

"Good morning, your ladyship. I trust you are suffering no ill effects from yesterday's trying journey?" she asked, smiling pleasantly.

"No more than usual. No more than usual, Missus—er Withers, is it?" her ladyship asked with obvious irritation.

"That's right. Mrs. Catherine Withers." Emmeline was trying to remain courteous and grateful for her ladyship's hospitality.

Lady Poole's vast bosom heaved with frustration. "Don't think you can bamboozle me, young lady. I know quality when I see it, and you've never done a day's work in your life." She waved a hand to silence Emmeline as she seemed about to interrupt. "As sure as I'm sitting here, you're running away from something. I know you won't admit it, but one thing I've a right to know. You've spent the night under my roof, and I want to know if you've committed any crime—anything the law might come after you about?"

Emmeline had tried to be calm, not to get angry and give herself away, but this was too much. "My lady, how dare you suggest such a thing? I've broken no laws and done nothing to harm anyone! And for you to make such accusations is quite intolerable. I thank you for a night's rest and sustenance, but that is all. My bag is already packed and I will leave immediately!"

She jumped up and moved quickly toward the door.

There was a roar from the bed. "Come back you little hothead! At once!"

Accustomed to obedience, Emmeline stopped and turned around.

"You heard me. Come back here. Sit down and stop being foolish." Lady Poole's expression was still ferocious, but there was a decided twinkle in her eyes. "I didn't accuse you of anything except running away, and I notice you didn't deny that." When Emmeline still didn't deny it, she went on. "Maybe I've made a muddle of it, but I've a suggestion to make that might just be in your best interests."

Emmeline had calmed down and was embarrassed by her hasty outburst. She was ready to listen to what Lady Poole had to suggest.

"You've probably wondered what Harriet's place is in this household. Well, she's m'cousin, once or twice removed, and her family left her without a penny, so I took her in some fifteen years or so ago. She's a sort of companion, but she earns her keep by looking after me. You know, helps me dress, fixes my hair, and so on." She looked at Emmeline shrewdly.

"I'm going to miss her for a week or two until she's back on her feet again. If you've run away, as I believe, there'll like as not be a hue and cry. Family looking for you. If you want to stay here until things quiet down a bit, live as family but help me the way Harriet usually does, then when she's up and about again I'll see you get a ride to a post house, and I'll even give you a reference to help you get a position—if that's what you're set on."

Emmeline still hadn't said a word. It sounded too good to be true.

Lady Poole smiled grimly, guessing what was going through her mind. "Stay until after lunch. Think about it. Go and talk to Harriet if you like. Then when we've had some lunch you can decide what you want to do."

Emmeline had one question now. "If I decide not to accept the position, will you stand by your offer yesterday to take me to the post house?"

Lady Poole glowered at her. "Of course I'll stand by it. I don't go back on my word, miss." She reached for a wrapper lying on the bed. "I'll see you in the dining room, one o'clock sharp."

EMMELINE RETURNED to the library, but Jane Austen was forgotten. She would have to talk to Harriet, of course, as she had a strong feeling that Lady Poole was a cantankerous old lady and not at all easy to work for. But it seemed like an opportunity she couldn't afford to miss. It was most unlikely that Charles, when he returned, would think to look for her so close to home, and she could make sure not to be seen in any public place.

It would also be good training, although she knew that governesses did not live as family as a rule. But working as Lady Poole's companion, she realized, would be vastly different to living at home as a daughter of the house. She would have to account for her time, would be unable to go riding or fishing or have very much time to herself at all.

She suddenly wondered if she would be able to keep the bedchamber she had used last night, or if she would be consigned to a cold room in the attic, and have to make her own bed and clean up after herself. She must make sure of that before agreeing to anything. When she'd had a governess her father had been alive, and she couldn't recall how the woman had lived, but thought it was somewhere between the two—not treated as a servant, but yet not one of the family.

It was all so difficult. The best thing would be to see Harriet if she was awake, and find out what she could tell her.

She returned to the chamber she had used last night, where the little maid was cleaning out the hearth and straightening up the room.

"Does Miss Harriet have a bedchamber on this floor?" she asked. "I'd like to visit her if she feels well enough to receive me."

The cheerful little maid jumped up. "Oh, yes, miss. Her rooms' just two doors away, and she's had breakfast already, so I'm sure you could peek in and see if she's awake."

After being pointed in the right direction, Emmeline found the door and knocked lightly. There was an answering, "Come in," and she entered a room almost identical to the one she'd just left. It flashed across her mind that Lady Poole's proposition had probably been in her head before they even reached the house yesterday and had influenced the choice of room even for the one night.

Harriet was looking comparatively comfortable, with some form of cage under the bedclothes which kept them away from her injured ankle. Like Lady Poole, she wore a wrap around her shoulders and a nightcap covered her hair.

She smiled warmly at Emmeline. "My dear Mrs. Withers, how kind of you to visit me and to give me the opportunity to thank you for all you did for me yesterday," she gushed quite sincerely.

"Don't even think about it, Harriet," Emmeline said quickly, but Harriet was not to be stopped so easily.

"Oh, but I must tell you what dear Dr. Matthews said when he saw how well you had bound up my ankle. He said, you're a very lucky lady, Miss Jones, to have had someone on the spot who knew what to do about this sprain. He also asked if you'd taken the shoe off before the swelling got too bad, and I told him you had cut it off."

"All I tried to do, Harriet, was to make you as comfortable as possible until a doctor could help you. If I succeeded, then that is all the thanks I need," Emmeline said firmly and, as Harriet tried to say more, she followed Lady Poole's example of putting an effective hand up to stop further argument.

"Now that I know you're coming along all right, I have a favor to ask of you, and, I might add, it is at Lady Poole's suggestion that I am come." Emmeline paused as Harriet looked questioningly at her. "Her ladyship has proposed that for the time of your incapacity, I should stay here and give her the kind of assistance you have always so ably given her."

"Oh, dear. I was wondering how her ladyship was going to get along while I'm unable to walk," Harriet murmured. "What is the favor?"

"Between now and luncheon, I am to decide whether or not it would suit me to spend a week or two here, helping her in your place. In order to made the decision, I need to know what the work involves, and how you feel about it." Emmeline saw fear enter the older woman's eyes, and hastened to reassure her. "Harriet, I can promise you one thing, for personal reasons which I cannot disclose, there is no possibility that I would stay any longer than the time it takes for you to be on your feet again."

"Thank you, ma'am. I was quite concerned about that," Harriet admitted. "But what do you want to know?"

"Why don't you start at the beginning of the day when you get up, and tell me what you do between then and going to bed," suggested Emmeline.

Harriet thought for a moment, and then began. "Suzy, the maid who helps me, wakens me with a cup of tea and brings me my hot water to wash. That's about seven o'clock. Then by the time I'm washed and dressed, she brings me my breakfast so that I can eat it before her ladyship wakens, which is usually about eight o'clock. You see, her ladyship has a bell that rings here in my bedchamber, and the minute I hear it I go to her right away, or she gets a little cross."

So that's why she was so grouchy this morning, thought Emmeline. She didn't have her personal slave to wait on her! Aloud she said, "I see. Then what do you do?"

"I ring for her maid to bring hot water and mend the fire, then I help her bathe and put on a clean nightcap before breakfast. While she's having breakfast I find out what she wants to wear that morning, and put it out ready for when she's finished eating. At that time I take the tray and place it outside the door for the maid to pick up."

Emmeline gave a reassuring nod, and said, "Go on."

"After I've helped her dress, I leave her alone for a while, and then I meet her at eleven o'clock in the morning room after she's met with the housekeeper, and she goes over any letters that have to be written, or any invitations she wants to accept. If we're going out in the afternoon, she usually tells me then and I get out whatever she wants to wear after lunch, and make sure that the carriage will be waiting."

"We always have lunch at one o'clock in the dining room, and after that either we go out, or her ladyship reads while I take care of the correspondence. She likes to take a rest at about three o'clock when we're home, so I help her out of her things and onto the bed, and an hour later when she rings, I go up and help her dress for dinner and fix her hair."

Emmeline put in, "After that you help her out of her things and into bed, I suppose."

"Oh, no." Harriet said. "If we're dining out, I go with her, or if we're entertaining I make sure everything's going all right. But the nights we stay in alone, she usually likes to play chess, or sometimes whist, for an hour or so."

"Is there anything else you do in your spare time, Harriet?" Emmeline was being sarcastic, but Harriet didn't even notice.

"Well, I check all her clothes before I put them away and send any downstairs that need to be repaired or washed." She thought for a moment. "And I go into town and change her library books once a week. Tom drives me in the carriage."

That's out, as far as I'm concerned, thought Emmeline. She knew she dare not show her face in that town.

"Is she a pleasant person to work for?" Emmeline thought she knew the answer, but asked all the same.

"Oh, Mrs. Withers, she's been such a wonderful person to me that anything I do for her is a pleasure. But she does get cross with me when I don't do things exactly the way she wants, I must admit."

Emmeline thanked Harriet, and made her way back to the library where she knew she would have privacy to think. If she were to succeed in getting a position as a governess, she knew she'd be looking after children from early in the morning until late at night. And, having had a governess, she had a pretty good idea of what the work entailed.

Now she had an insight into the work involved as a companion or, more particularly, as a companion to a woman who was too clutch-fisted to pay for an abigail's services as well. For two or three weeks it would be invaluable experience, and if at the end of that time she was able to get a reference from Lady Poole, it could make a deal of difference in her chances of securing a good position.

Six

Emmeline entered the dining room on the exact stroke of one, but a second behind Lady Poole. Two places were set, neither at the head of the table, so she stayed back to see which one her ladyship took before moving toward the other.

The luncheon was light, simple, and quite good, and she followed her ladyship's example of concentrating on the food, assuming she preferred to have their discussion later.

At the conclusion of the meal, Lady Poole placed her serviette on the table and noisily cleared her throat.

"I assume you have reached some decision regarding our earlier discussion, Mrs. Withers?"

"Yes, your ladyship, I have." Emmeline paused to select her words carefully. "I would be willing to accept the position for the duration of Harriet's incapacity, but with some exceptions to the duties she presently performs."

"I might have known," her ladyship said crossly. "All right, tell me what they are and I'll see if they're tolerable."

Looking directly at her, Emmeline proceeded to list the things she would not do. "I would not be prepared to go to town, to exchange your library books or to do anything else there; I would not accompany you on visits to people in the neighborhood; I would reserve the right to absent myself from any gathering here after perusing the guest list; and, although we are not kin, I would still expect to have all the privileges your cousin now enjoys."

It was impossible for Emmeline to tell from the closed expression on Lady Poole's face whether she was going to accept her terms or not. What she didn't expect was the sudden chortle that seemed to come from the depths below her ladyship's vast bosom.

Far from annoying her, the first part of Emmeline's ultimatum seemed to be a source of amusement and also triumph, judging by the gleam in her eyes.

"Very interesting, young lady. Very interesting indeed." Her ladyship chortled again. "So you're afraid of being recognized, in town or by our local society." She saw Emmeline's quiet nod in the affirmative, and became serious once more. "You needn't fret yourself. I'd much rather no one recognize you myself or I'd be without help, wouldn't I?"

She paused, giving Emmeline a long look before dealing with the remaining points. "As to the other, you'll work for me and do as I say, and you'll not answer me back the way you did this morning. There'll be none of that. But you'll be treated as what I'm sure you are—a lady. Does that satisfy you?"

"Yes, my lady. It completely satisfies me," Emmeline said, much relieved that there was to be no further argument.

"Now, what do I usually do at this hour?" Lady Poole demanded.

"You usually read until about the hour of three, if you're not going out." Emmeline had clearly memorized the schedule since her talk with Harriet.

Lady Poole nodded approvingly. "Or if I don't decide to do something else, which is just what I'm going to do today. We'll take a look through the invitations and such and see which need replies. And by the way, I've no intention of calling a chit like you missus. You say your name's Catherine, so that's what you'll go by. Now get me the envelopes from the salver in the morning room, please."

By the end of the day, when she'd tucked Lady Poole neatly into bed and sent the maid away with garments to be cleaned, pressed, or repaired, Emmeline was glad to drop into her own bed with a book to read until she fell asleep.

But a pair of silver-gray eyes with thick black brows kept coming between her and the pages of the book. She hoped his father's health had improved because if he died, what she'd done would be completely unpardonable, and she now knew she wanted his forgiveness. It had been cowardly of her to run away, and she wouldn't have done it had he not put the idea into her head. But it was too late—she couldn't go back now. Even if she could get back before his return, he'd hear of her departure from the butler anyway. And then he might even beat her, if what her mother had said was true, and she couldn't tolerate that.

On the table beside her bed was the prayer book her father had given her as a little girl, and between its pages was a pink rose she had pressed as a souvenir of Charles's proposal under the rose bower in the garden at Grantley Range. At least he had been honest, and admitted that he did not love her. She reached for the book, opening the page at the flower, and pressed it to her lips. If only he'd had just a little feeling for her, she would have tried to make the best of it and would not have left, but his cruel words still hurt.

Even after she put down the book and snuffed the candle, the thought of him disturbed her sleep. Her father would have been ashamed of her, she was sure, as he'd tried to teach her to meet life head on, the way he'd taught her to ride, and at the very first obstacle she'd turned tail and run. She could almost see his reproachful eyes.

EMMELINE WAS AN earlier riser than Harriet, and was up long before the maid was due, so she tugged on the bell pull, hoping there was someone on duty. Suzy was at the door within a few minutes with a morning cup of tea and hot water to wash in. Breakfast followed quickly, and left her with more than half an hour to herself before Lady Poole would need her.

She'd solved the problem of the bell pull from Lady Poole's bedchamber to Harriet's by getting a pair of strong footmen to switch the furniture, including a protesting Harriet and her bed, from one bedchamber to the other. The two rooms were identical, and when the move had been accomplished, it was impossible to tell from the inside that a change had been made at all.

It seemed no time at all before a loud ringing indicated that Lady Poole was awake. Emmeline moved swiftly along the corridor to her ladyship's room, and once there she rang for her maid. The old lady looked strangely vulnerable sitting up in bed with her nightcap crooked and sleep still in her eyes. Emmeline had never known a grandmother, but she could easily believe that she'd have looked just like her ladyship did now.

"What are you smiling about, Catherine?" she grunted. "I'm not sure I like smiles at this hour of the morning."

"You wouldn't like my face to look like this, would you, your ladyship?" she asked, scrunching her face up until it was all glares and grimaces.

That brought a laugh from Lady Poole, which was what Emmeline had been aiming for, and she did the rest of her duties swiftly and cheerfully. Finding it easier to arrange someone else's hair than her own, she dressed the thinning gray locks so that small wispy curls peeked out from under the sides of the lace cap and framed her face.

And so began a period that became nearer four weeks than the two to three originally planned, as Harriet feigned pain in her ankle in order to have a longer rest. Emmeline guessed what Harriet was doing, but hadn't the heart to blame her. The work was tiring even to someone as young as herself, for Lady Poole was used to being waited on continuously, and even her approval had a gruff, demanding ring to it.

To say Emmeline was unhappy would not have been true, but she had to learn to curb her temper, hold her tongue, and suffer through indignities which would not have been inflicted upon her had the guests of Lady Poole had any idea who she was. She consoled herself with the realization that the people who were rude to her were usually parvenus and cits.

When entertaining for tea, Lady Poole always asked Emmeline to pour for, though she would never admit it, her hands had become unsteady of late. One particular afternoon an old rival of her ladyship's, Lady Davenport, came to call, bringing with her two granddaughters whom she planned to bring out in London the next Season. The young ladies were not more than eighteen years old, and neither of them was pretty, one inclining to be short and a little too plump, and the other tall and rather awkward and angular.

Lady Davenport's piercing eyes had assessed the new addition to Lady Poole's household, understandably unsure of the position Emmeline occupied. Emmeline so far outshone her granddaughters both in appearance and composure that she gave the lady cause for concern, and she made a point of asking Lady Poole who the young woman was.

"Catherine? She's the granddaughter of an old beau

of mine. Pretty little thing, ain't she? Just helping me out until Harriet's back on her feet again." Lady Poole gave a gleeful chuckle at her deception.

Naturally, this did nothing to allay Lady Davenport's fears that no one would notice her own chicks while Emmeline was around, the fact that there were no young men in the room notwithstanding. On the pretext of desiring a second cup of tea, she came over to the tea table where Emmeline sat, waited until the tea had been poured and was being handed to her, then deliberately jerked the saucer, spilling the scalding tea over Emmeline's lap.

The move was most effective in getting Emmeline out of the room, as she had not only to change her clothes, but also to apply a soothing cream to her thighs which stung from the scald.

Emmeline knew it had been done deliberately, for she had seen the look Lady Davenport gave her as she grabbed at the saucer. She was not surprised when later that day, Lady Poole brought up the incident again.

"I hope you learned a lesson today, Catherine?"

Emmeline's eyes widened in question, not understanding the reference at first.

"When you hand a cup you always hold it away from you, preferably over the table or the floor, particularly when you're pouring for an old hand like that Davenport woman. She's practiced that trick until she has it perfected, as long as she's dealing with a green girl." Her eyes softened. "Did it burn your legs?"

Now Emmeline understood. "Not badly. They just smart a little. I'm not so green that I didn't know it was deliberate, your ladyship. But what had I done to her? I'd not said a single word to her up until then."

Lady Poole's derisive cackle was aimed at her rival and not at Emmeline. "You were too pretty by far. You made her girls look like frights by comparison. I, for one, tried hard but failed to find an attractive feature in either one of them."

"Was Lady Davenport very beautiful in her youth, ma'am?"

"She was quite a dazzler, but nothing compared to me. You wouldn't believe it now, to look at me, but I was exquisite when I came out. An incomparable. And what a time I had—the balls, the theaters, the beautiful gowns." Her eyes became misted with the precious memories. "You haven't had a Season yet, have you, Catherine?"

"No, ma'am, my father died just when my older sister was about to be presented. I . . ." She stopped, realizing that she'd already said too much.

Lady Poole's eyes held a look of interest, but she did not pursue the matter further.

On occasion, sons or husbands accompanied Lady Poole's callers, and though her wedding band proved not to be the deterrent she had hoped, Emmeline's cool manner kept most of the young men at a distance. The older men were more experienced and paid her attention only when they could catch her alone for a moment, and this she soon realized and took precautions to avoid.

More troublesome to her were their ladies, who became jealous and blamed her for attracting the men's attention. Though they said nothing in front of Lady Poole, when her ladyship was at the other end of the room they took the opportunity to make unpleasant remarks about Emmeline, even saying things to her face.

Because of this she took to quietly removing herself from the drawing room whenever there were any male callers, and though Lady Poole made no comment, Emmeline had the feeling that she was aware of her reasons. She also started to wear her less attractive gowns for company, and drew her hair back quite severely. This made her look more like hired help, and some of the more shrewish ladies became demanding and tried to give her orders, but the ony person she took directions from was Lady Poole. If a cit became difficult, she left the company and attended to one of the many tasks awaiting her attention in another room.

She actually came to be quite fond of Lady Poole, to understand her bouts of bad temper, and to learn how to cope with them without letting them hurt her. She had to behave, for her ladyship would tolerate no insubordination, but she developed first a respect for the bad-tempered old lady and finally a kind of affection. She would be sorry, in a way, when Harriet was on her feet again, and she would have to leave the security of this house and make her way alone in an outside world of which she had begun to be a little uncertain. She knew now that not everyone welcomed an attractive young woman into their midst, and many that did had dreadful motives.

Seven

Lord Charles Carruthers found his father almost at death's door, but as had happened before, the presence of his son did much to help the marquess's spirits, and within a couple of days a vast improvement could be seen. After a further two days the doctor pronounced him no longer in danger. Charles sent a message to Emmeline, advising her that he would be delayed for more than the three or four days he originally anticipated. He had no way of knowing she was no longer there to receive it.

He described her in detail to his mother and father, and both were very anxious to meet her, the marquess even more so because of her resemblance to her late father, but until his health improved it was not considered wise to bring her for a visit.

On the sixth day Charles decided he could safely leave for Warwickshire, and set out early in the morning. The closer he got to his home, the more he looked forward to seeing Emmeline and having the opportunity of getting to know her better. He would shortly have a delightful surprise for her, which might make up somewhat for his extremely inconsiderate behavior so soon after the wedding, for which he had been feeling deep regret.

When Jenkins met him in the hall and showed him

the note that she had left only a few hours after his own departure, he flew into a rage, and it was fortunate that she could not see the results of her broken promise. Jenkins had not suspected that she had run away, as he assumed her reference to visiting friends to be true, but Charles assured him that she had no friends in the area, and in fact had never been out of Yorkshire in her life.

To try to trace her after she had been gone almost a week would be almost impossible, and when he thought of what could befall an eighteen-year-old innocent in the streets of London, he went almost out of his mind with worry.

But it was already quite late in the afternoon when he arrived home, and nothing much could be done that night. He sat down to an early dinner and then tried to map out a plan of action in an effort to at least give the impossible a try. After a while there was a knocking on the door, and Jenkins came in to announce the unexpected visit of two dear and trusted friends, Sir John Barrington and Lord Nigel Morton. Charles welcomed them, swore them to absolute secrecy, and told them what had happened. Gladly he accepted their efforts of help in finding Emmeline, and the trio sat down in earnest to plan their campaign.

Three days later, after having inquired at all the post houses and inns in every direction, personally examined the lists of passengers on all the stagecoaches that had passed through the area in the last week, and even secured the names and descriptions of all the people who had hired post chaises in the vicinity, they were forced to conclude that she had disappeared into thin air.

Leaving his friends to keep searching for local clues, Charles made the long journey back to Yorkshire, in case Emmeline had somehow managed to return to Grantley Range. But there they had neither seen nor heard anything of her, and Lady Barrow seemed not to care as a mother should, but only insofar as it affected her own interests. Lord Barrow, however, was furious when he heard of her departure and seemed to take it as a personal insult to himself.

Feeling by turn angry and frustrated, Charles realized there was nothing he could do but return to Warwickshire and see if the detectives Sir John had traveled to London to hire had come up with anything.

Exactly three weeks after Emmeline's departure, the three friends reluctantly gathered together over a gloomy dinner. They bitterly agreed that all they could do now was leave it to the detectives who, having already tried all the employment agencies without success, were now searching the underworld of London for someone answering her description.

It was a day or so later that Lord Nigel Morton happened to be home when his mother was entertaining some of her friends to tea. He was a good-looking man, well liked by both young and old, and they were delighted when he joined their party. He had just stepped out onto the terrace for some fresh air when he heard the conversation change to a discussion of a neighbor of his acquaintance, Lady Poole.

"Just fancy, the old girl is so clutch-fisted that she won't even pay an abigail. She's used that old cousin of hers as abigail and companion for a dozen or more years."

"Well, the poor thing can't do much for her at the moment. Didn't you hear? A wheel came off Lady Poole's carriage about three weeks ago and poor Harriet was thrown out. She was lucky to get away with nothing more than a sprained ankle. Of course, Lady Poole was uninjured, as it would take more than a broken wheel to get her out of the carriage once she'd been wedged in," a voice he did not recognize remarked unkindly.

"Didn't you see the pretty young widow who's helping out while the cousin's laid up? Lovely child, very ladylike, with the most beautiful pale blond hair and eyes of the deepest blue, but so sad to be widowed at her age. She's bound to make old Harriet jealous, the way she's been fixing her ladyship's hair. The way it just peeks out from under her lace cap is most becoming."

The ladies went on to talk of other things while Sir Nigel started to piece together the extraordinary conversation he had just heard. They had said the cousin's accident had occurred about three weeks ago, so the timing was right, and the description certainly seemed to fit.

When his mother was finally alone, he asked her if she might be visiting Poole House at any time in the near future, and she told him that she too was curious about the young companion. To her delight he volunteered to escort her on her impending call at the house, which was planned for three days hence.

Emmeline was still accustomed to assisting Lady Poole in entertaining lady callers, but now when they were accompanied by young men she would quietly disappear until after they left. She had no wish to complicate things further by their showing an interest in her.

On this particular day, she was seated at the tea table and had poured for Lady Poole's visitors, all ladies. Lord Nigel and his mother, however, arrived a little after the others, and he got a glimpse of Emmeline before she saw him and left the room. He didn't dare ask any questions in case she should overhear and become suspicious, but he felt it very possible that the young lady was, in fact, Charles's runaway bride.

As soon as he had taken his mother home, he rode over to see his friend Carruthers and told him of the encounter, describing in detail the temporary member of Lady Poole's household.

"She was sitting at the tea table when we first entered the room and despite the severe style, I could see how lovely her hair must be. But those eyes! Huge and bright as sapphires, with the most extraordinary dark brows and lashes. I know what I'd like to do if I was married to her." Lord Nigel was obviously smitten.

"I know what I plan to do if it really turns out to be Emmeline, and when I've finished with her she won't sit down at a tea table or anything else for a week, I promise you," Charles said grimly. "I'm very much afraid it will turn out to be a false lead, however."

But he agreed it warranted investigation, and decided to make a call on Lady Poole the next day, while Lord Nigel kept the house under surveillance in case it was her and she should see him and try to run again.

At twelve noon, Lady Poole's butler admitted Lord Charles Carruthers to the drawing room and went to find Lady Poole, who was alone at the time, having sent Emmeline to the kitchen to change the menu for luncheon.

Since Charles was the grandson of a very dear old friend of hers, Lady Poole was delighted to receive him, and went immediately to the drawing room to greet him.

After the barest civilities, he came straight to the point. "Lady Poole, I have reason to believe that you are harboring a young lady in this house who happens to be my wife, Lady Emmeline," he said sternly.

"You mean to say it was you the little fool ran away from, Charles?" the old lady asked in amazement. "Don't accuse me of harboring her, though. Protecting would be more like it, for if I hadn't persuaded her to help me out she'd be in some hellhole in London by now. Not a doubt about it." Lady Poole was more than a little put out by the accusation.

"That has been my worst fear, Lady Poole, for these past two weeks and more. She left while I was visiting at Lord Millford's bedside," he told her, tremendously relieved that Emmeline was safe. But with the relief came an almost uncontrollable fury and a desire to ring that pretty little neck. It was with some difficulty that he maintained a polite and pleasant conversation with his hostess.

"I was not aware that Emmeline had any friends in the area, Lady Poole," Charles remarked as calmly as he could. "Have you known her long?"

She gave a snort. "Ever since our coach wheel came off on our way back from our annual trip to Bath. I can never sleep well in those wretched inns, so we were making an early start."

"I would not have credited you with picking up strange young ladies on the highway, my lady," he offered, anxious to hear all the details.

"That I don't. I'm not yet let in the attic, young man," she affirmed testily. "M'cousin was hurt and Catherine, as she called herself, came walking along and offered help. When I saw she was a lady, and a young one at that, I tried to find out who she was, but she'd tell me nothing. She had some harebrained idea of going to London to secure a position, so she told me."

He had an idea. "Would you do me a favor, Lady Poole, that is, in addition to what you have done already? Would you explain a little to her of what would probably have happened to her had she reached London alone?"

She grunted. "Wouldn't believe you, eh? I'll make a start on it and you can go on from there. By the time we've finished, I doubt she'll try that idea again."

She reached for a bell pull, and when a footman came she told him to ask Mrs. Withers to join them.

"I trust your father's health is now improved, Charles?" her ladyship asked.

"Thank you, ma'am, somewhat. At least he is presently out of danger," Charles replied.

EMMELINE WAS TALKING to Cook and changing the luncheon menu from thinly sliced salmon with capers, back to the original order of cold tongue and ham, and smoothing ruffled feathers as much as she could. She was wondering if Lady Poole, who had been in a particularly contentious mood all morning, might be feeling a little under the weather but be too obstinate to admit it. There had been one or two occasions of late, when she thought she was not being observed, that Lady Poole had allowed herself to give way to a wince of something very much like pain. Emmeline would have to find some way to ease whatever problem the old lady had, without letting her know she'd been found out.

When the footman told her she was wanted in the drawing room, she did not at first think there might be company, as it was a strange hour for anyone to call. Rather, she thought, her ladyship had changed her mind once again and wanted something entirely different for her lunch.

Wearing a pleasant smile, she walked into the drawing room and across to her ladyship. "What can I do for you, ma'am?" she asked with a familiar twinkle.

Lady Poole was looking reproachful. "You can drop a curtsy to our guest, my lady." She nodded toward a spot behind Emmelne's left shoulder.

Emmeline swung quickly around and was holding her skirts in readiness before she saw him. She froze, eyes wide open with shock and fear. "My lord," she whispered, then sank into the deepest of curtsies, her head lowered to hide her embarrassed face.

Charles reached for her left hand to help her rise, and his fingers touched his wedding ring which she had continued to wear. 'Yes, Emmeline, I am your lord, but it would seem you have forgotten that you're my lady." His voice held barely controlled anger, and Emmeline felt a tremor of fear.

Lady Poole cleared her throat nosily, and Emmeline turned toward her as if seeking protection, her hand still in Charles's grasp.

"I'll have a maid pack your things—or would you rather do it yourself, Emmeline?" The gruffness in her voice betrayed the old lady's emotions.

"My wife," Charles paused at the word, "my wife is not leaving this room except with me. I'd appreciate your first suggestion, Lady Poole."

When a girl had been dispatched, eyes big with curiosity, to pack all the things in Emmeline's bedchamber, Charles turned once more to Lady Poole.

"I can never thank you enough, ma'am, for keeping her safe from harm. If I can be of service to you at any time, you only have to ask and it will be my pleasure to return the favor." He released Emmeline's hand for a moment to take the wrinkled one of the old lady and bring it to his lips.

It seemed there was something in Lady Poole's eye, as she rubbed it hard. "I've enjoyed having the chit around me, and I'll warrant she's learned a few things she didn't know before. But I'd not have kept her with me if I'd known who she was, you have my word on it." She swung her gaze to Emmeline. "And as for you, young lady, I've something to tell you before you leave.

"You've obviously no notion what happens to young ladies who take themselves off to London without friends or anyone to turn to. His lordship probably knows more about it than I do, but I'll tell you one thing, girl, they don't get hired as governesses or companions, nor even scullery maids, when they have faces as pretty as yours. It's too much of a temptation to husbands and sons, so only hatchet-faced spinsters with a few gray hairs and a lot more years than you have are hired, and then only with the best of references.

"I'm sure his lordship can tell you more than I can about the men and women who hang around post houses and cheap lodgings in London, waiting for innocent young things just up from the country. If they can't persuade them to go along with them, they take 'em by force, so I'm told." Her ladyship looked grim, and Emmeline's eyes grew wide with horror.

Charles briefly took pity on her. "I think she's beginning to understand, your ladyship. Let's not frighten her further," he murmured, but not without some satisfaction.

The old lady's face screwed up into a smile. "Well, my dear, if you're ever allowed out again, which should be in two or three years by my reckoning, you may come and visit me. For now, you may kiss my cheek."

Emmeline bent to touch her lips to the wizened cheek, and Lady Poole's arms came around her and hugged for a moment.

The maid entered with Emmeline's bag, which Charles picked up. With a bow to Lady Poole he took Emmeline's arm and in silence they walked out to the waiting carriage. After helping her inside, he entered also and sat facing her. One peek up from her downcast eyes showed her only cold fury in his, so she eased herself into the corner farthest away from him. She felt herself start to tremble and was ashamed of her cowardice.

Aware that he had noticed her trembling, she tried to speak, but her voice came out a hoarse croak. "What are you going to do with me, my lord?"

He looked at her in silence, then gave a deep sigh. "At the moment I haven't decided." His eyes bored into her as he continued. "When I returned home and discovered you'd broken your promise to me, my first desire was to find you and give you a thrashing you'd never forget. Then I went up north to see if you'd returned to your stepfather, and he begged for that privilege as soon as you were found."

"You're taking me back to him?" she asked, her voice barely audible.

"No, I'm not. You're my wife now, and I'll handle things my way," he said grimly.

She was not sure which was worse, being handed over to her stepfather again or facing the wrath of the stranger she'd married.

"When we reach the house, I want you to behave as though you'd just been away on a visit, as you indicated to Jenkins. The servants, with the exception of Jenkins, know nothing of your running off—and I'd rather keep it that way," he continued. "You will go directly to your room and stay there until I come, or send for you. If you attempt to leave the room without my permission, you'll be very sorry, I can assure you."

He needn't worry, she thought. She had no intention of trying to run from him again, no matter what he did to her. But it was more than fear that had set her trembling. The touch of his hand had sent little waves of warmth through her arm. If he would permit it, and not make life too unbearable once he got over his anger, she would stay this time and make the best of it.

"I will, of course, want to know later what happened to you from the time you left this house until you came under the care of Lady Poole. For now I have just one question. Did you meet anyone else on the road besides her ladyship and her cousin?" The stern eyes bored into her, and he seemed to be deeply interested in her answer.

"No. It was dark when I left, and I went through the woods and out onto the main road. I walked for more than an hour, and Lady Poole's broken carriage was the first thing I saw. It was very early in the morning," she said, trying to make him understand why there was no one about.

"And you did not become too friendly with the staff at Poole House?" he asked gravely.

"No, sir, not at all. I had dealings with the housekeeper, the cook, and the maids, of course, but Lady Poole agreed that I should live as family," Emmeline assured him. "Of course, I worked hard and Lady Poole was very strict, but she was very good to me in her way."

He nodded, seemingly in deep thought.

"Give me your reticule. I assume all the money you have is in it?" he asked, as she silently handed it to him. "On second thought, don't bother answering that. I wouldn't believe a word you said anyway."

She felt her cheeks burn with shame, knowing his words were deserved, and was glad he couldn't see her face clearly in the dimly lit carriage.

"Fifteen pounds," he counted. "I'll keep this to cover some of the expense of searching for you. Where is the sapphire ring, and your other jewelry?"

"I left your ring in the bedchamber, in a drawer. I only have my pearls and my grandmama's ring," she whispered. "Please don't take them from me."

He held out his hand without answering, and slowly she took off her right glove and removed a small diamond and garnet ring, which she dropped into his hand.

"I'll keep it until you can be trusted not to pawn

it—if such a time is ever reached. You may also bring the pearls to me when you have unpacked."

The carriage had turned into the driveway, and in a few minutes the old house came into view. She was hardly aware of being helped down as, with a hand under her elbow, he swept her inside, through the hall, and up the stairs. At the door to her bedchamber, he paused, then reached across to open it. "Don't forget. You do not move out of here until I tell you," he growled softly, as he pushed her quite gently inside and closed the door behind her.

She heard his footsteps continue along the corridor, then she went over to the vaguely familiar bed and sat on the edge. He hadn't locked the door. There was no need, since she was trembling so much she couldn't have walked any further without aid.

Eight

A fire had been lit in the bedchamber and was burning cheerfully. Now, as the darkness gathered, Emmeline warmed her hands before it, then took a taper and lit a candle by the bed that had seemed so large when she had first entered the chamber some four weeks ago. She had been too tired then, and later too intent on leaving, to notice what an attractive room it was. Peach and apple green predominated in the draperies and hangings both around the bed and at the windows, and the carpet echoed the colors. It was a woman's room, the chairs and chaise being daintily proportioned and covered in a warm peach velvet.

Now, she also noticed the fragrance of dried lavender that emanated from the bed linens, refreshing the entire chamber.

She didn't expect to see Charles for several hours. From his stern tone and demeanor when he left her, she was sure he would leave her to dwell at length on her misbehavior and her punishment.

Nor did she believe anyone else would come. Hunger pangs had now started to add to her discomfort, as she had only eaten a small piece of toast for breakfast, and had been whisked away from Poole House before luncheon was served. In her mind she had no doubt at all that she would be deprived of supper, and she even thought wistfully of the dry bread and water her stepfather used to send to her room when she had misbehaved.

To take her thoughts away from her immediate problems, she unpacked the small bag she had traveled with, and put away the sober clothes that were not really as suitable for employment as a governess as she had thought. She placed her pearls on a table, then took the sapphire ring from the drawer where she had left it and put it with the pearls. Busy at the task, she didn't hear the first knock on the door, and started nervously when the second, louder knock sounded. A young maid entered with a tray of covered dishes.

"His lordship said to bring your supper, milady," the curious girl said. "There's bread, potato soup, fenelle of fish, and partridge pie, and the chef will have some sweets and ices ready when you ring for them."

"What is your name?" Emmeline asked the girl.

"Betty, milady."

"Thank you, Betty. Just put the tray over here on the table and I'll serve myself."

When the door closed behind the maid, Emmeline stood for a moment, trying to hold back grateful tears that threatened to squeeze out of her tightly closed lids. Perhaps Charles was not quite so angry with her as she thought. She did justice to the excellently prepared meal, savoring the delicacy of both the fish and the partridge, and a summon on the bell pull brought Betty again with ices and sweets. When everything was cleared away, she sat on the bed once more, and wondered what her husband was doing and what he had in store for her.

She didn't have long to wonder, as a peremptory knock sounded and Charles entered through the inside door of the chamber. He was wearing a wine-colored brocade dressing gown, and she noticed how magnificent he looked in such informal attire.

"Thank you for allowing me to have supper, my lord," she said. Her voice was stronger now, and he turned to look sharply at her, then seemed to realize that she was sincere in her thanks.

"Did you think I would not, Emmeline?"

"My stepfather used to send up dry bread and water when I misbehaved, and even that was better than nothing."

He remembered her rising from the table that evening when her stepfather ordered her to his study, and knew that the fear in her eyes had not been caused by a spell in her room on bread and water.

"He hurt you, didn't he?"

"Yes. He whipped me on several occasions." She was starting to tremble again and now couldn't look at him anymore. He's asking about the past so as to decide what to do with me now, she thought.

Then she felt his hand on her shoulder, drawing her toward him, one hand under her chin, gently making her look at him.

"Don't tremble, little one." His voice was deep and soothing. "I have decided that whatever the reason you left, it was not entirely your fault. I must take a share of the blame. You won't try to run away again, will you?"

Emmeline found it difficult to believe he could be so kind and understanding after what she'd done, but needed his assurance and trust in her again. "No, not if you'll let me stay," she whispered. "And I don't have my fingers crossed this time."

His smile brought good-humored creases around his eyes. "I must remember to watch your fingers when I exact promises from you in the future."

As his glance caught the jewelry on the table, he reached into a pocket and produced her grandmother's ring. "I'm sure I don't need to keep this any longer," he said, and placed a kiss in the palm of her hand before closing her fingers on the ring. Then he steered her toward the fireplace, and sat beside her on the chaise, his arm still around her.

Only when he could feel her begin to relax against him did he start to talk. "I've been agonizing over the reason you ran away. Did I put the idea into your head, or had you planned it already?"

He waited patiently for some time, then turned her face toward him and was not surprised to see her pink, embarrassed cheeks. She still hesitated, but his look encouraged her. "I hadn't planned to do so, but it seemed a good idea when you mentioned it."

He reached for her hands and spread the fingers out on her lap, at which she lowered her head and muttered, "I know you will never believe me again, but I am not lying, my lord."

Pressed so closely to him, she could feel his deep sigh. "Did Lady Barrow talk to you before our marriage, my love?"

"Oh yes," was the prompt reply. "Sometimes I thought she'd never stop. She talked about the wedding, and how I had to say my vows good and loud—but I couldn't when it came to it. And she talked of how happy she was that Agatha would now be able to go to London for the Season."

His eyes narrowed at her last remark, but he asked only, "Did she not tell you of a husband's desires, and the duties of a wife?"

This time she turned to face him, her eyebrows puckered in bewilderment. Slowly she nodded.

"She did, but I'm very sure she didn't mean for me to tell you about it."

"I'd much prefer that you not start with any preconceived notions about marriage. I think you'd better tell me what she said, whether or not she meant you to. She need never know that you have told me, my dear."

Emmeline gulped: "She said that I was to make the most of your being romantic before the wedding, as afterward there would be no more of it, and you'd be much sterner than my stepfather had been."

He was looking at her with eyebrows raised slightly. "And did you believe that?" he asked.

"Not at first. Not until it started happening . . ." she began, turning away from him.

"Go on," he said. "You don't have to look at me if it's easier this way. What did I do—or not do?" One of his hands was stroking the back of her neck in a comforting way.

"You left me to ride alone in the carriage for that awfully long trip, and even when you came inside for a while, you wouldn't talk to me," she said.

"You're quite right about that. I gave you little thought because I preferred to ride horseback rather than in a coach. I was doing a lot of thinking, mostly about my father, and also about my last conversation with Lord Barrow, but I had no right to leave you alone all that time. Of course you became upset." His voice was soft and apologetic. "And then I was rough with you, and threatened to lock you in your room for days. No wonder you ran away. It would have been surprising if you'd stayed."

His head bent toward her and his lips gently caressed her cheek, then moved lower until they were able to capture hers. His tongue made gentle forays inside her mouth, then moved away, leaving her gasping but not wanting him to stop.

"Did your mother say anything about . . ." He paused, trying to think of an inoffensive word he could use, but having some trouble for he'd not needed one for years.

"Bedding me?" she suggested tentatively.

For a moment he sounded as though he was about to choke, then he managed to mutter, "Yes."

"She said I shouldn't and wouldn't enjoy it if I was a lady, and it was best to lie still and think of going to the dressmaker and ordering a new gown. By the time I got to the first fitting she said you'd have finished and be back in your own bed."

Now Charles really was choking, and Emmeline had to leave her comfortable position and pat his back until he could breathe properly again.

"She said that the marriage was an arranged one and that you probably kept a woman for the pleasure part of it, and would just use me to produce an heir," Emmeline went on.

He sighed heavily. "And then my angry words served to confirm it. No wonder you ran off, Emmeline. Please forgive me, my dear, for none of it is true. That old agreement was worthless, as your mother knew very well. Did she tell you anything at all about what happens?" he asked hopefully. He had no experience at initiating virgins.

"Not really. Just that it was painful and very distasteful," she said. "Was she not telling the truth?"

He placed his hands on her shoulders. "Emmeline, your mama was probably telling the truth insofar as she feels about it. But it doesn't have to be that way and I don't want it to be that way between you and me. Can you try to forget your mama's ideas, and let me try to show you the way it should be?"

"I'll try, Charles," she said, with a newfound trust in his goodness.

"I'll leave you to disrobe and prepare yourself for bed. Do you think you can manage it yourself this once, or should I ring for a maid to assist you?"

"I never had anyone to assist me at home, my lord, nor at Lady Poole's, but then I never had a gown with such awkward buttons in the back." She had no notion of how bewitching her hesitant smile was.

"Turn around. You'll soon learn that this also is one of the things husbands are useful for."

His large fingers fumbled with the tiny buttons, but at last they were unfastened and she held the gown up in the front, embarrassed at her dishabille.

"Now, I'll allow you fifteen minutes before I return. Take your hair down for me and brush it smooth. I have an urge to see its length."

Left alone, Emmeline allowed the dress to drop to the floor, then removed her undergarments. In the chiffonier she found a lacy nightdress and a matching robe her mother had selected, then she sat down at the dressing table to brush out her golden hair.

That was the way Charles found her when he returned to the room a little later. He crossed to where she sat, took the brush from her hand, and gently passed it through her hair in long, even strokes.

Emmeline felt a strange warmth spread throughout her body as she watched his reflection in the mirror, and when he laid down the brush and drew her up and into his arms, she came willingly, as though in a dream.

His lips found hers once more, and she eagerly opened her mouth to taste the remembered flavor of his tongue, then parry it with her own. Still holding her in a firm embrace with one hand, his other hand now began to learn her body, stroking it gently from the top of her spine, around each shoulder blade, spanning her narrow waist and then slowly circling each buttock and molding her closer to him.

She had thought it impossible to feel any more alive than at this moment, but as his hand slid up her side until it reached the gentle round of her breast, she gasped with surprise and a pleasure that was immediately surpassed when the soothing fingers reached the bud at the center and gently caressed it to a pointed hardness.

As he changed hands and stroked the other side, her arms seemed to move of their own volition to reach out and touch him, feeling for the most sensitive places until the clothing they had no more need of lay in a heap around their feet.

Picking her up in his arms, he carried her to the bed where the covers were already turned back. Gratified by her response, he continued to caress and be caressed in turn until his gently searching fingers found the moistness he had hoped for.

"Don't be frightened, my love. This will hurt a little, but just this first time," he promised. Something did hurt, and she couldn't hold back a little whimper, but then she felt movement and a strange feeling of excitement started to build deep inside her.

She fell asleep in his arms, exhausted after this exciting culmination of the events of the day, and woke just after dawn, wondering what she was doing lying next to someone until she saw the outline of his beautiful body and the handsome face which, in peaceful slumber, looked much younger.

She wanted to wake him, yet wanted to watch him sleep, and while she was thinking about it his eyes opened and he looked at her the way he had looked last night.

"How do you feel, my love? Did I make you sore?" he asked softly.

"Oh, no," she said quickly, denying the tenderness she had felt upon waking.

He reached for her and she was as ready as he to relive the wonder of the night before. And as he had promised, this time the sharp hurt was no longer there.

His eyes crinkled in a warm grin. "Did you ever reach the first fitting of that gown your mama suggested?"

The dimples appeared as she laughed out loud, then

became serious. "I'm so sorry Mama never felt like this. It's so much better than being a lady."

He stopped her talking to steal a long, slow kiss.

"I was going to suggest a ride around the estate this morning, but I think you'd better put on a gown and we'll go for a drive. I know that despite your protests, you are a little sore. Before we leave, though, I want you to see the stables."

She would have enjoyed an early morning gallop, but knew he was right and it should be postponed a day.

He returned to his room, leaving the connecting door open. She heard him dismiss his valet, and as soon as she was ready they went down to breakfast together.

In her opinion a visit to the stables was not made in a gown, but he had seemed anxious that she see them this morning, so she made no demur.

His grays were being harnessed, but she saw the big black stallion he hunted with, and despite Charles's warning, she fed him sugar and crooned to him until he was accustomed to her voice and smell.

As she went from stall to stall, she realized he had a stable to easily rival theirs when her father was alive, and she looked forward to spending much time here if Charles would permit it. As she came to the last two stalls, she heard a familiar nicker. In one stood Thunder, and in the other Lovely Lady, both looking in prime condition and very happy to see her.

Emmeline's tears began to flow as she gave them the last of the sugar she had brought along, and she leaned her forehead against an upright, trying to regain control.

"Here, my love," Charles said, slipping a handkerchief into her hand and turning her head into his shoulder. "Cry it out of your system, and you'll feel better." One of his hands massaged her back while the other held her close, and the tears gradually subsided.

"He sold them to you?" she asked, loudly blowing her nose.

"No. He sold them separately to a farmer and a squire, and I had to pay through the nose to get them for you, but it was more than worth it to make you happy. I determined to get them for you the day I came back and saw your anguish at their loss."

"Charles, you are so good to me. I promise I'll never forget, and I'll try my best to be the kind of wife you'll be proud of." She stood on tiptoe and lifted her face, but he still had to bend his head to give her a comforting kiss.

Still holding her close, he kissed the tip of her nose and teased, "I didn't know I was marrying a watering pot."

"I never cry. I don't know what's happening to me lately," she said between sniffs, and was rewarded with a warm hug.

She was still sniffing, however, when he introduced her to Bart, his head groom, who appeared to know all about the two horses.

"We'll take good care of them, your ladyship," he assured her. "They're two beauties, but they weren't in such good shape when they first arrived. Some people don't appreciate good horseflesh when they see it."

Emmeline turned questioning eyes to Charles, and he confirmed, "I bought them, and Bart brought them down here just before the wedding, and it was only just in time. Fortunately, there was no permanent damage done."

It was a very serious Emmeline who walked over to the curricle and allowed herself to be helped up. She realized that Charles had shown more kindness to her in just a few weeks than she'd known in two years. He might not love her, but she'd try to show him in every way she could how grateful she was for everything he did. She had learned a lot at Lady Poole's, and she knew she could be a far better wife and helpmate than her mother had ever been.

THEY STARTED OUT in the opposite direction to the one she had taken almost a month ago, passing through a small village where the men they met doffed their caps and the women gave little bobs. She could not but admire the way Charles handled the ribbons and they traveled at a fast clip, except when he paused to point out one of his tenant farms, or a herd of his Herefords grazing.

In one small town she saw Lady Davenport coming out of a drapery shop with her two granddaughters, and Emmeline had the pleasure of cutting her dead. Charles had seemed to be on the point of stopping the curricle, but she put a gloved hand on his arm and asked, "Please don't stop. It would be very difficult."

He chuckled. "I assume you have already met Lady Davenport."

"Yes, and as she attempted to do me an injury, I have no wish to be introduced as your wife."

"It won't become a problem, as I have not socialized very much here. My father and mother have tried to persuade me to stay at our London house each Season for a number of years, and on the few occasions that I do, I attend enough balls and parties to last for the rest of the year."

Emmeline became quiet at the mention of his mother and father, then asked, "Do they know that we are wed?"

"Of course they do. I told them I was about to get leg-shackled, and then I told them the deed had been accomplished, but I did not tell them I had lost my bride. They are most anxious to meet you, but I don't think a prolonged visit would be a good idea until my father is feeling a little stronger."

"I imagine the marchioness is very severe and proper. What if she doesn't like me?"

He placed his free hand on her knee for a moment. "She will love you on sight. Don't have any qualms about that."

They had turned around and were heading back to the house for lunch when Charles asked her to explain a little of the events at home that had made her decide she must leave Grantley Range.

"It's a little difficult to explain, but I'll try. Being the middle child isn't easy in most families, but my father always made me feel very special because I looked like him. It was for him that I became such a tomboy. When he died, I felt cheated. I was just sixteen and I was working hard at my lessons and trying to please him in every way. Then suddenly he was gone and I was left alone.

"I felt resentful that first year when the family was in mourning. He'd never minded my riding astride and wearing breeches, and so I wore them and rode every day for hours, and I know I was mourning him in my own way much more than Mama and Agatha were in their dark clothes and impatience about missing balls and Agatha's Season. It was then I first realized they didn't love me because I could not be like them. Then Lord Barrow started to call on mother, and though he tried not to let it show, he despised me from the start. I was too young to be able to hide my dislike of him, and when they were married Mother gave him full permission to chastise me and try to turn me into a lady like Agatha."

He smiled grimly at that. "I'm glad they didn't succeed in making you in that mold. Please continue."

"Before I even met you, I wanted to leave home

desperately and I'd saved up some money, but then you came along and offered me a chance to get away. Poor Agatha was so jealous she tried to tear my hair out, then wouldn't speak to me, but Mama became less critical and seemed almost pleased with me at last."

They were nearly home now, passing the lake fringed at the far side with sycamore trees. Charles was still silent.

"I feel I did a lot of growing up at Lady Poole's. I didn't mind the work because I liked her, grumpy as she was at times. And she made me behave, but she was fair."

"I've noticed a difference in you. But it would have come about without your running away. I think that just getting out of that house helped you," he said. "I'm glad you talked so frankly. It has enabled me to understand you and your reasons much more. If you can talk to me so freely, we've already come a long way."

They drove in a companionable silence until they were quite close to the house, when Emmeline spoke again. "I know it sounds silly, but would you drive directly to the stables? I'd like to take another look at Thunder and Lovely Lady. I can't quite believe they're really here."

The boy held the grays while Charles helped her down, and then they both went to take another look at her old friends. After a few minutes she turned to go to the house, and slipped her hand in his.

"Thank you for being so understanding, my lord," she whispered.

"I'll be much more understanding if you'll try harder to call me Charles," he said, giving her hand a squeeze.

Nine

Luncheon was barely adequate, and breakfast had been quite unappetitizing to Emmeline's taste. This had surprised her in view of the excellent dinner she had eaten last night. She determined to put what Lady Poole had taught her about household management to good use and made a mental note to inspect the kitchens tomorrow and see about some improvements.

Dinner was once again superb, and she enjoyed eating in the elegant dining room with Charles. At his suggestion he brought his port into the drawing room rather than drink it in solitary state, and they talked of the future while Emmeline worked out a design to make tapestry seat covers for the rather shabby dining chairs.

"We have the good fortune, as newlyweds, of not having to entertain for some time," Charles remarked with satisfaction. "It will give you a chance to get the staff in shape, with the cooperation of Jenkins. I realize that my frequent absences have made them somewhat lazy."

"Will you still have occasion to travel a great deal, Charles?" Emmeline asked, hoping it would not be too frequent.

"Not as much as before, but I try to cover both my own and my father's estates and it takes up a little time." He watched her carefully as he said, "I shall be here for several days yet, but then I am very much afraid I'll be gone for a sennight. Do you think you'll be all right?"

She looked hurt. "I gave you my promise, my lord," she said, and then flushed as she remembered having given it to him before. With a sigh she brought both hands in full view and mouthed, "I promise," with a wry grin.

Although Charles did not wish her to do so when he was away, they mounted and joined the local hunt one morning. Emmeline rode Thunder sidesaddle, but still made a very good showing, being in at the finish. Charles had promised her she could have more breeches made, but styled a little fuller and more feminine, and could ride astride as long as she did not leave the estate wearing them.

Their lovemaking brought them warmth and passion each night, and they spent the better part of each day together, getting to know each other, and thus enjoyed a delightful week before he had to leave.

Emmeline's visits to the kitchen had revealed a first-class French chef who prepared nothing except dinners, and a very mediocre cook who made breakfast and luncheon. Both had been inherited with the property. The two of them constantly quarreled, which was evidently the reason for the poor quality of the meals early in the day, and Emmeline decided to give the cook the chance to improve. If not, she would have to let her go. She didn't want to start marriage with the unpleasant problem of finding a new cook, but was determined to do so if it became necessary

She was a little disappointed by Charles's farewell, as he pecked lightly on her cheek after breakfast and ran out without a backward glance, but they had enjoyed a long and passionate farewell in their bedchamber much earlier. He'd already given her his direction in case an emergency arose, but she was hoping she would not need it, as she would not like to have to call him back because of her youthful inadequacy.

The rose garden was her favorite spot, and while Charles was away she spent hours memorizing their names, snipping dead flowerheads, and learning which roses were perfumed heavily and which had not much smell at all, but had long-lasting blossoms. It was the best time of year for roses, and she always had a bowl in the drawing room and also one in her bedchamber.

The herb garden needed much work, and she had to weed it herself as the gardener had no interest in it and was always pulling up the plants instead of the weeds. At home there had been a particularly attractive and useful herb garden, and she worked diligently to plan one on similar lines, being fortunate in finding a book on the subject in Charles's library.

In the house, she explored the rooms and found that many of the unused chambers were quite dusty and ill-kept. She spoke to Charles's agent, and he secured a couple of girls from the village to help the maids clean and polish throughout, and a sewing woman to repair the bed and table linens, which were also in poor condition.

When Charles had been gone only three days, she had already made inroads into the work that needed to be done. She felt tired but proud of her industry, although when she went to bed for the third lonely night she had some misgivings about the morrow, a premonition of sorts. It kept her awake for some time, until she determinedly put it aside, telling herself it was just anxiety—she was trying too hard.

"Easy, boy," Emmeline murmured softly as she patted Thunder's neck. "I know you want a gallop, but it's far too hazardous on this wretched saddle. It won't be long now, and then we can ride like the wind the way we used to."

The day had dawned bright and sunny, and Emmeline was enjoying her early morning ride on Thunder. She had ridden Lovely Lady yesterday, so as to keep them both exercised, and for the time being, under duress, she rode sidesaddle, with a groom in attendance. Charles had requested that she take a groom with her while he was away, as she was not yet familiar with the estate, and she would not disobey his wishes.

This morning she was expecting a dressmaker from the nearest town, and in addition to other garments, the seamstress was to make several pairs of wide riding breeches. Charles had informed her that this particular person was the soul of discretion and that no one outside the estate would ever see her unusual riding attire.

On her return to the house, she went direcly to the kitchen to oversee the labors of the staff. Since she had complained, there had been an infinitesimal improvement in the breakfasts, but no change in the quality of the luncheons. It was obvious that no more than one cook was needed, and she knew which one would have to go, but was awaiting Charles's return before taking the necessary steps.

Jenkins found her there a half hour later, going over the stocks of various foods with the housekeeper.

"Pardon, your ladyship. A dressmaker person, a Miss Bridges, is here with several bolts of fabric. Where would your ladyship wish her to wait?"

Emmeline hid a smile. Something about the way Jenkins identified the woman gave her reason to believe Miss Bridges might be something more than a little dressmaker.

"Thank you, Jenkins, I'm going to my bedchamber directly. I will see her there in ten minutes, and you may have the fabrics brought to my chamber also." She smiled a dismissal.

Unfailingly deferential to her, Jenkins still conveyed an almost disapproving formality. Unlike most of the staff, he had not been inherited with the house, but had been a footman at Charles's home when he was growing up. She wondered how long it would take him to forgive her for running away from his master.

Miss Bridges proved to be a woman in her forties, or at least that was the age Emmeline guessed her to be. She was most attractive in a rather obvious way, and dressed more fashionably than anyone she could recall ever having seen, but then Emmeline had not yet been to London.

Charles felt that the gowns her mother had purchased for her were good enough only for the country when they were not entertaining, and he wanted her to select some more day wear and, of course, the riding breeches. It was his intention to help choose her gowns for dinners and balls on his return next week. He had also mentioned that when they arrived in London for the Season she would immediately order a complete new wardrobe.

Her ears still burned from his blistering comments when she told him that her wedding gown was ordered with a view to trimming it later for evening use.

The first thing that caught Emmeline's eye was a bolt of sapphire blue velvet, and she absently stroked the luxurious fabric while Miss Bridges took her measurements.

"Isn't it lovely, your ladyship, and surely meant for you," said Miss Bridges. The astute dressmaker had ascertained Emmeline's coloring before making the trip. "A riding habit, I believe. Let me show you some styles."

This time Emmeline was most interested in being

outfitted, as she wanted to look her best beside Charles, who was himself so very handsome. She ordered a dress of a deep gold stiff cotton that enhanced her pale gold hair unbelievably, and this would be trimmed in matching lace and turquoise ribbon, made with gored panels to give a little more fullness. A delicate peach jaconet muslin was to have straw-colored lace around the neck and at the hem; and then another carriage dress was to be made in deep green bombazine, this time with pale gold silk ribbon for trim. And all were to be made with the new hemline, an inch or so above the ankle, which Miss Bridges was wearing and, she assured her, was being worn by all the fashionable ladies in London.

Miss Bridges made notes to obtain gloves, bonnets, reticules, and shawls in the colors Emmeline had chosen, and then they came to the garments dearest to Emmeline's heart.

"When I met with his lordship, he informed me that you wished me to design a garment for you to ride in, your ladyship. Was I correct in believing he was referring to a form of breeches?" Miss Bridges's puzzled frown was followed by a disapproving stare as Emmeline nodded, smiling faintly.

"You were quite correct, and I have given it so very much thought that I believe I can sketch for you something similar to what I want." With a few swift strokes on the paper Miss Bridges was using, Emmeline outlined a pair of breeches that fit comfortably close around the waist and hips, but with legs that flared toward the ankle, giving the appearance when standing of an extremely narrow skirt.

Miss Bridges was an intelligent woman with an eye to business. When she saw that Lady Emmeline was determined to wear such an unusual garment, she made a few suggestions of her own, a tuck here and a pleat there, and the final design, although still a trouser, had a pleat at the center back and front to make it look even more like a skirt than before.

Without it being too noticeable, she used all her powers of persuasion to try to induce Emmeline to order more gowns, but when she saw she was wasting her time, she took her leave, arranging to return in two days for a first fitting.

IN CHARLES'S ABSENCE Emmeline would have much preferred to have her meals served in her bedchamber rather than eat alone in the formal dining room. But Charles, anticipating that she might want to do this, had insisted that she maintain the formalities, if only to keep the servants on their toes. Accordingly, she had dressed for dinner each evening, and was doing so once again with Betty's assistance when, through the open window, she heard a commotion below. For a brief moment her heart leaped, thinking it must be Charles returning earlier than he planned, but when a knock came on her door and Betty showed Jenkins in, she was forced to hide her disappointment.

Emmeline was at her dressing table where Betty had been putting final touches to her hair. "Yes, Jenkins," she inquired.

"There's a gentleman arrived, your ladyship, who says he's your father, by the name of Lord Barrow."

She looked at Jenkins through the mirror and her hand went to her mouth to try to stop her gasp at this unpleasant news. She looked away, but not soon enough to hide the fear in her eyes. Jenkins's impassive face gave no indication of the surprise he must have felt at his mistress's reaction.

But when she turned around and looked once more at the butler, she had controlled her fears and her face was as emotionless as his. "Lord Barrow is my stepfather, Jenkins," she corrected with quiet dignity. "Is he traveling alone?"

"Yes, your ladyship, except for his man. He has luggage with him."

Emmeline heaved a sigh of resignation. "It's most unfortunate that Lord Charles is not at home. Give him the green room in the west wing, and inform him that dinner will be served in one hour."

"Very well, milady." With a slight bow he turned to go.

He was almost at the door when Emmeline remembered. "Oh, and Jenkins," she called, "please let Phillipe know that dinner will be delayed."

"Yes, your ladyship." Jenkins cleared his throat. "Did you wish to make any additions to the menu for the gentleman?"

Emmeline's smile was almost malicious. In Charles's absence she had reduced the number of dishes served at the meals she had to eat alone. "No, Jenkins. Lord Barrow cannot expect a more elaborate meal at such short notice."

Emmeline had to admit to herself that she was not trying to make less work for Phillipe, the chef. She knew the frenzy of activity in the kitchen that adding more dishes at this hour would have entailed, but would have ordered it nonetheless had the guest been anyone but her stepfather. She knew, too, that had her mother and sisters accompanied him, she would have immediately gone down to greet them and personally attend to their comfort.

"Did you wish to change your gown, your ladyship, now that your father's here?" Betty was a cheerful girl, always anxious to please, and never minding extra work.

"Stepfather," Emmeline corrected her, a little too emphatically, "and, no, this gown is quite suitable, but you may get me my cream shawl." It was not a cold evening, but she had an unaccountable reluctance to display her bare shoulders to Lord Barrow.

She dismissed Betty, but remained seated at the dressing table, looking at her reflection. He would see some changes in her, she felt sure. The face that looked back at her in the mirror was calmer, less impetuous than that of the girl who had lived with her family in Yorkshire. What she couldn't see tonight, in her anxiety about spending the evening alone with a man she'd always hated, was the way her face had recently been reflecting a glow of happiness not felt since her father's death. Even she noticed, however, that her eyes suddenly looked haunted. Why couldn't Charles have been home, she silently asked her reflection.

A little before the hour, she left her bedchamber and gracefully descended the wide staircase. At her approach a footman opened the door to the dining room and she entered, walking directly over to the table to check, as usual, that everything was as it should be. As she reached the heavy oak sideboard, there was a tap on the door and Jenkins entered.

"Beg pardon, your ladyship. Lord Barrow asked that you join him in the drawing room for refreshments." For once he looked quite disturbed, realizing that for a guest to countermand orders was most unusual.

"Did you tell him that I would meet him in the dining room, as I asked, Jenkins?" Emmeline had become very quiet, reluctant to have a conflict with her stepfather, but determined not to let him take charge in her home.

"I did, milady. But when he came down he went to the drawing room and ordered sherry." He was floundering in deep water, not sure of what to do. "Perhaps it would be best if you join him."

A spark of anger lit her eyes, but Emmeline's voice was still quiet. "When I desire your advice, I will ask you for it, Jenkins. You may tell Lord Barrow that I am awaiting him here, and then instruct the kitchen to start serving whether or not our guest is seated."

She stood by the chair at the head of the table, usually occupied by her husband, and inclined her head for Jenkins to seat her before he left the room.

Her stepfather waited a full five minutes before joining her. It was Emmeline's belief that he had been imbibing for some time before he started to drink sherry in the drawing room. His usually pale face was considerably flushed, and he swung around as the footmen entered with the food before he had taken his place.

"Good evening, sir. I trust you had a comfortable journey. Your visit was unexpected." She spoke in the way she might have addressed a stranger at her table.

"I see marriage has little improved your disposition, my girl," he said, bristling with anger. "You're as disobedient as ever."

"In my house, my lord, I give the orders, and I expect guests to comply with them." She nodded to the footman to start serving the fish.

Lord Barrow was by now almost livid, and he sent glares around the table and sideboard, his angry eyes searching for something. Emmeline watched him, waiting for him to try asking a servant to bring him wine, but apparently he thought better of it.

"Is your husband so cheap, ma'am, that he doesn't serve wine with his food?" he asked with a sneer.

"On the contrary, Lord Charles keeps an excellent cellar, I believe, but as I rarely touch wine, I was waiting to find out the type you would prefer." Emmeline's lips froze into something not quite a smile.

He named several French wines which meant nothing to her, but she nodded to Jenkins, who left for the wine cellar.

With a full glass in front of him, and obviously enjoying the well-prepared food, Lord Barrow's high color lessened somewhat as he concentrated on the meal. Emmeline saw him glance at the sideboard once or twice to see if there were any other dishes there that had not been proffered, but seeing none, he held his tongue.

When only three types of sweets were served, he could keep silent no longer. "Seems to me you married a penny pincher, Emmeline. Not a lot of variety in the other courses, and a very poor selection of sweets."

"There was an ample selection of food for the one person for whom dinner was prepared. Had you let us know of your intention to call, I can assure you there would have been a great many more choices." And I would have escaped to Lady Poole's for a day or two, she thought.

"You've become most impertinent since you left home. Do you speak to Lord Charles this way?" he asked in a waspish tone.

When Emmeline, realizing the servants would have gossip for months to come, didn't deign to answer him, he touched his glass for more wine. Behind his back she could see Jenkins pointing to the brandy decanter.

"Would you not prefer a fine brandy, my lord?" she suggested, hoping to have an excuse for leaving him alone, but he anticipated her thoughts.

"Only if you stay and have your tea in here with me. I've more to say to you before you retire for the night."

His truculent tone was reason enough for her to leave, but she would not let him know she still feared him.

"Jenkins, please bring Lord Barrow the brandy decanter, and I will have the tea tray now, in here."

She sat back in her chair and waited while her stepfather poured himself a generous measure, took a large swig, and then smacked his lips in satisfaction.

"So, you let us spend a fortune on all those new gowns and a white church wedding, and then when you got down here you ran off. I'll warrant he made your sides smart when he got you back here," Lord Barrow said spitefully.

Emmeline didn't consider his remarks worthy of contradiction even though she knew all had been paid for by Charles. Her silence, however, served to make him the more unpleasant.

"Tanned your hide, I'll wager, by the way he looked when he came to Grantley Range." He gave her a look of pure hatred, and Emmeline rose in an attempt to stop him seeing the shudder that shook her body. She had never been alone with him before when he was drunk.

"If this is the conversation you wished to have with me, I believe I will forgo tea and say good night to you, sir," she said coldly. "When did you say you would be leaving?"

"I didn't say, you uppity miss, but I'm not going till my son-in-law returns." As she passed his chair, he grabbed her wrist in a painful grip. "You still didn't tell me if you got what you deserved from his lordship."

"If you're asking if I was punished, sir, the answer is no. Lord Charles is not that kind of a gentleman."

She took advantage of the door opening to yank her wrist out of his grasp. Jenkins's impassivity was being sorely tested as he and a footman entered with the tea tray.

"You may bring that to my bedchamber, Jenkins," she said, sweeping past him.

Safely in her room, she sipped the tea and tried to remember all the things she'd said to her stepfather. She knew she had been very rude, and she was likely to get a scold from Charles for treating a guest in such a manner, but she hadn't been able to help herself. The next problem was how to avoid him until Charles's return.

Betty had been alerted by Jenkins, and helped her out of her clothes and into a nightgown and wrap, but she was far too tense to get into bed just yet, so she stretched out on the chaise and reached for a book.

THE CRASH OF the door as it was swung wide brought Emmeline to her feet. Lord Barrow stood in the opening, looking malevolent, a heavy horsewhip in his hand. As if in a tableau, he stood perfectly still for a moment. Then, loudly cursing her, he stormed into the room, slamming the door closed behind him.

The bell pull was near the bed, and Emmeline edged toward it and gave it a sharp tug. Lord Barrow was almost on top of her, holding the whip raised, but he had been drinking and was not as fast on his feet as she was. With a quick twist she dodged behind him and ran toward the door, but this time she was not quick enough. He swung around and the heavy whip came down across her back and buttocks, causing excruciating pain, but her impetus carried her to the door.

She was only vaguely aware through the raw, burning sensation that he was shouting obscenities at her. She saw him swing the whip once more and knew she couldn't get out of its way. But suddenly the door opened and strong hands pulled her into the hall before the lash could once again reach its target.

In the confusion that followed, Jenkins and two of the large footmen effectively subdued Lord Barrow and hustled him out of her chamber and down the corridor, but not before she heard him shout, "I'll be back later to finish the job."

While the footmen took Lord Barrow to his bedchamber, Jenkins summoned Betty. He expressed a strong desire to evict Lord Barrow from the premises, but Emmeline would not give the order immediately. The morning would be soon enough to make that decision. She did, however, give instructions that her stepfather was not to be allowed near her chamber again. His last drunken words still rang in her ears, and she was afraid.

The pain in her back was so fearsome that Emmeline accepted a potion of weakened laudanum. After applying a soothing ointment to the ugly, bleeding welt, Betty went into the dressing room, where a bed had been made up for her so she could stay within call.

Emmeline slept fitfully, and the following morning, after giving the matter grave thought, she decided to request her stepfather to leave, and if he refused Jenkins and the footmen could do whatever became necessary.

Even with Betty's aid, dressing and walking down the staircase was agonizingly painful, and she paused for some time outside the dining room to allow a disconcerting dizziness to pass. She found Lord Barrow partaking of a hearty breakfast despite the fact that he was obviously suffering the effects of the previous night's overindulgence. He glared and grunted a good morning as she entered the room. By prior arrangement Jenkins dismissed the footmen attending the table, and waited just outside the door in case of trouble.

She came straight to the point. "In view of last night's disturbance, my lord, I have decided it would be best if you visit us in the future only when my husband is at home, and I must request that you leave as soon as you and your servant are finished with breakfast."

She looked him in the eyes as she spoke, and watched with fascination as his face turned from an unusual paleness to a suffused, florid hue as his fury became apparent.

"Don't you dare speak like that to your father, you uppity miss!" he shouted, an ugly expression on his face. "I'll stay just as long as I please, and you'd better be sure there's no repeat of last night's meager dinner, or I'll know the reason why!"

He had risen to his feet and started toward her, but stopped as Jenkins appeared in the doorway, backed by two burly footmen.

Ignoring his outburst, Emmeline stood her ground and continued quietly, "I would prefer that you leave of your own accord, my lord, but if necessary, I've no doubt Jenkins will be more than able to assist you."

Lord Barrow knew when to back down. He swaggered over to the door, then turned to face Emmeline once more.

"I'm leaving, but don't imagine for one moment this will be the end of it. By the time I've finished, you and your fancy husband will be the laughing stock of the *ton*," he promised with an unpleasant sneer. "You'll rue this day, mark my words."

Ten

Lord Charles was returning home after a particularly exhausting week. Because of his wish to spend more time with Emmeline, in this short trip he had tried to take care of a great deal more than he would have normally attempted. He had to keep a close eye on both his own properties and those of his father, since for some time now the marquess had been unable to get around without extreme discomfort. Of late, however, Charles had encountered seemingly insurmountable problems. There was much unrest in the country as groups banded together to protest the corn laws and urge their repeal. Only the thorough training his father had given him in his earlier years had enabled him to keep his tenant farmers happy and leave each property in good shape. He had left them also in good hands, as he had started a program of hiring capable managers, paying a little more than usual to get them, and then letting them assume more of the responsibility.

He rode quietly into the stable, wearily dismounted, and gave his horse into Bart's care. For once he ignored the head groom's obvious wish to talk. He was anxious to get cleaned up, see Emmeline, and rest a little before dinner.

Entering through the back of the house and using the service stairs, he reached his bedchamber without meeting a soul. In the next room he could hear female voices, and then the sound of the door to the hall closing. He was just starting toward the connecting door when his valet came in, so he decided not to disturb whatever Emmeline was doing in her bedchamber at this hour. He was dirty and much preferred that she not see him in this state.

"Hot water will be here, your lordship, in just a few minutes," his man said. Then, not knowing whether his master had spoken to anyone, he asked, "Is her ladyship recovered?"

"Recovered? You mean she's been ill?" Charles looked toward the connecting door, but as there was no longer any sound from the next room he turned back to the valet. "She's probably gone downstairs. I'll see her when I'm a pleasanter sight."

But the valet was not to be put off. He had heard gossip belowstairs, and was anxious to be the first to inform his lordship. "Seems to be some mystery, your lordship, if you'll pardon my saying so. It appears her ladyship's stepfather, Lord Barrow, arrived a few days ago, and had to be forcibly removed from her bedchamber."

With quick strides Lord Charles reached the connecting door and, finding it locked, knocked loudly, but there was no sound. "Emmeline," he called, "open this door at once."

There was movement in the room, then her voice answered, "Charles, you're back?" A moment later the door was flung open.

"What is all this about, Emmeline?" he asked, not realizing in his anxiety how abrupt he sounded. "You know I don't like you to lock these doors."

She retreated into her room, and Charles dismissed his valet and followed her.

"Please don't be angry, Charles. I had no choice in

the matter. My stepfather was here and I forgot to unlock it once he was gone," she began. As he came toward her, she retreated one more step and he noticed her wince as her back touched the bedpost.

In an instant his arms were around her. "What has happened, my love?" he asked gently as she struggled to hold back tears of relief.

"He got drunk and went berserk with his whip. Jenkins saved me just in time, and the next day I ordered him from the house."

"What!" Charles was furious, though not with her. "He didn't hit you, did he?" he asked, taking her by the shoulders and looking deeply into her eyes.

"He tried, but only one blow landed," she told him as he sat on the bed and pulled her into his arms.

"Now tell me everything that happened," he said to her.

"You'll never know how glad I am to see you," she said in a choked voice. "It was late at night, and he was roaring drunk. When he said he'd be back, Jenkins found the key in your chamber, and I thought it best to keep the doors locked until he left. I didn't realize that one was still locked."

She proceeded to tell him everything, not even omitting her rudeness at dinner that first night, but Charles would have none of it. It was her house, and her stepfather was the one who was being rude! Of course she agreed with him.

He cursed softly as he examined the ugly weal, which was healing under Betty's care, and then he turned up her face to his and kissed her long and lovingly. Her arms reached around his neck, and the horror of that night receded.

She didn't tell Charles of her stepfather's threat, as she didn't want to make him angry again.

"I should be ashamed to touch you with the dirt of

the road still on me," he said finally, showing not the slightest remorse. "I'll bathe and change, and then we're both going to have dinner in this room. I'll make all the arrangements."

Emmeline lay on the chaise and fell into a sleep deeper than she'd had for many a day. When she awoke, it was to find a light cover over her, and Charles, wearing a chocolate-colored silk dressing gown, supervising the addition of a sideboard and a small table to her chamber. Then an assortment of dishes was taken from footmen at the door and put into position by Jenkins.

When all was in place, Charles piled a chair high with feather pillows for Emmeline's comfort.

Jenkins's eyes revealed the pleasure he derived from personally serving the delicious dinner to his master and mistress. Emmeline ate in much the way she used to, feeling like herself once more, and even sipping the wine that Charles poured for her.

Replete and happy from the wine and the huge meal she'd just eaten, Emmeline sat back and watched her husband as Jenkins poured him a brandy. How could it be that so soon after their marriage her whole world righted itself the minute he returned? Perhaps if she were to have a baby he would grow to love her as the mother of his child? But then again, he might dislike her when she became fat and ugly.

"Did you get your breeches from the dressmaker?" he asked with a broad grin. "You should have seen her face when I told her what you wanted."

"We designed something between us that I don't think you will find too offensive. However, I didn't feel very well when she came back to fit me, and she had to be turned away." She gave a deep, frustrated sigh. "There were so many things, Charles, that I had started to do when you were away, and then that horrible man arrived and ruined everything."

"Never mind, my dear. You'll finish them soon, and we'll have the dressmaker come back again. What sort of things had you started?"

"Oh, supervising the cleaning of some of the empty rooms, the repair of linens, and going over supplies with Mrs. Carter. That cook has to go—the breakfasts and luncheons are no better. I started my herb garden, and, you see, I was just behaving like a good wife should."

His smile was soft and tender. "You want to be a good wife, don't you, Emmie?"

"Very much, my lord," she said, pleased that he'd shortened her name to that which her father had always used.

"Then you will be, I'm sure. Don't worry about the cook. I'll get rid of her for you." There was a pause. "How would you like to move to the townhouse in London for the Season?" He watched her face light up with delighted surprise.

"Can we? And you'll take me to see plays and attend balls, and get vouchers for Almack's?"

Her excitement made him beam at her indulgently. "Yes, little one, we'll do all those things and much more. Most of the clothes you have now, you'll leave here, and we'll start afresh with a complete new wardrobe for the Season."

"You mean I won't be able to wear the gowns Miss Bridges is making?" He saw the disappointment on her face.

"You'll take them with you to wear en route, for I've a fancy to show you off a little before we settle in London. You see, my grandmama will be the only member of my family who will be in town this Season, so I believe we should first pay a visit to my mother and also to my sister."

"How soon will we have to leave, Charles?"

"Oh, not for about a month, I would think," he replied thoughtfully. "How soon can you be ready?"

"Would tomorrow be all right?" she asked with a show of pretty dimples.

"Now that's what I like to see. That's the first time those dimples have appeared since I returned."

"Mama said they were disgusting and that it wasn't ladylike to smile so broadly." He growled, and the dimples came back. Then she realized with dismay what the visits would mean. "Suppose your family doesn't like me? What will you do? They may feel they should have seen me first, before we were married."

"Will you stop being such a ninnyhammer, Emmie, and take my word for it that they really will love you. My sister's home is nearest, so I think we'll go there first, and then on to my parents' home. It will help give you a little town bronze ahead of time."

"Oh, yes, I'm sure it will be good for me," she said ruefully.

"Do you know what I'd like to do to you just now, but can't as I'm afraid of hurting you?" he asked, deep regret mirrored in his eyes.

"Yes" she whispered, "I know, and it's what I'd like, too. It's not nearly as painful as it was. I'm sure it would be all right." She dropped her eyes from his and studied the lapels of his dressing gown as her cheeks flushed in embarrassment.

"I'm beginning to understand what your governess meant when she said you absorb knowledge like a sponge. You've had so much thrown at you since we married, and yet you remember it all, and are looking for more. I believe it would be more enjoyable, however, if we waited another day."

Charles was much more tired than he realized, and it was not long before Emmeline persuaded him to go to bed. He retired to his own bedchamber without too much argument.

She had been in the habit of leaving a candle lit during the night in case she needed to call Betty, and tonight she went to sleep in the same way. It must have been the early hours of the morning when she awoke to find Charles standing by her bed, leaning over her.

"Just checking to see that you're all right, my love," he said, tucking the sheets in carefully. "You must have had a bad dream."

He bent to kiss her and ran a finger on her flushed cheek. "Go back to sleep," he murmured, and left the room.

"THEY'RE AMAZING," CHARLES said pensively, watching her as she spun around to show him the back view. "But how will they feel when you're mounted? Will the fullness get in the way?"

"That's what I'm about to find out, sir," she told him, blushing under his smiling scrutiny. "I was planning to take out Thunder this morning and see how they feel." She was unaware of the anxiety in her look as she asked, "Would you have time to join me, Charles?"

"But, of course," Charles murmured, with a wicked grin. "I wouldn't miss the sight of Bart's face, and the rest of the grooms and stable hands when they see you mount astride."

With brows raised above dancing eyes, she asked, "You wouldn't want to see me fall, surely, my lord?"

He stood up, his own eyes mocking. "Not really, my love," he assured her with a lazy smile. "But if you are going to be so clumsy, I'd rather my arms were there to catch you. Can you be ready in thirty minutes?"

Emmeline was as yet too careless of her appearance

to take much time dressing for riding. She was, however, a little anxious about the new breeches. The worst thing that could happen was that the seam in the seat might split.

As they approached the stables, Charles reached for her hand, squeezed it, then held it firmly in his. He had not sent word for the horses to be readied, as they would be expecting to use the sidesaddle for Emmeline.

"Good morning, Bart," he said pleasantly. "Saddle up Ulysses for me and Thunder for her ladyship. She will be riding astride today, not sidesaddle."

Judging by his expression, Bart had assumed her ladyship was not riding today when he saw she was wearing what he thought was a straight skirt, but he'd been serving the gentry all his life, and he just shook his head slightly as he went to give the orders.

When Thunder was led out, Emmeline went over to him to adjust the stirrups, and his lordship was close behind her. She mounted with ease and felt no give in the seams.

"Feel good?" his lordship asked with a grin.

"Very good indeed." She sighed with relief, then bent closer so that only he could hear. "But it's most surprising how much work suddenly needs to be done out here. The boys and grooms have never been so anxious to sweep." With a show of great industry, at least a dozen grooms and stable boys were wielding brooms and rakes whereas five minutes ago the yard had been completely empty.

Emmeline was happy to remain silent at first as they rode together once more. She was enjoying the freedom from the cumbersome skirts and awkward position ladies were expected to assume when riding. Thunder was enjoying it, too, for she was closer to him and her knees gave better control. But she began to wonder what might be the cause of Charles's silence.

"You are very quiet, Charles," she remarked.

"Not really. I just thought you might prefer to commune once more with your horse. He seems to like it much better this way, and we both know that any moment you are going to break into a gallop." He looked appraisingly at the picture horse and rider made. "I have never seen a woman ride so well, and very few men, I must admit."

She accepted the compliment with a smile and gracefully inclined her head. "We both thank you, sir."

There was a large oak tree in the distance, and Emmeline pointed to it with her crop. "Shall we?" she asked.

"By all means. Do you want me to give you ten lengths?" he taunted, grinning widely.

"Certainly not!" she said, with a proud lift of her head. "On the count of three. One, two, three!"

They were neck and neck at first, then she slowly edged forward, and as they reached the tree she was still no more than half a length ahead, but it was enough.

They could hear the ripple of a stream nearby, and Emmeline turned toward it, Charles staying at her side. When they reached a clearing, he warned, "Don't dismount until I tell you, as I want to be there in case of problems."

She was about to protest, but thought better of it and waited until he tied his horse to a tree and came over. He stood back, allowing her to dismount without help, but when the heel of her boot caught in the hem of the breeches leg, he quickly stepped forward and saved her from a fall.

After thanking him, she insisted on mounting again to try to see what had caused her to trip. This time they both saw what the problem was. "I think they need to be about an inch shorter, Charles," she said, pointing out where the fabric caught on the heel. "You see, if they were just that bit shorter they couldn't catch."

He agreed, helped her down again, and they sat on the bank of the streams, his arm about her and her head resting on his shoulder.

"You still miss Lord Grantley very much, Emmie, don't you? He must have been a very good father."

"He was the best of fathers! He never once hit any of us, but just one word of reproof from him and I wanted to crawl into a hole and die. I keep thinking that he must be glad that I married his friend's son." She frowned. "He does know, don't you think?"

"I'm sure he does. And now you will have his friend for a father-in-law. Try not to worry about any of my family liking you. The clothes we picked out will look well on you, and it's always so much easier when one knows one is dressed right." He looked down at her breeches. "I'm afraid these will have to be left behind, my love, but you'll be able to wear them on your return."

"You know, Charles, the only time I have ever really thought I was dressed right was when Mama and Agatha went out and selected all those clothes before the wedding. They seemed so sure about the styles and fabrics in fashion. And now I know that they're really not good enough, are they?" She gave a philosophical shrug.

"I happen to know that you took no part in their selection, so I cannot offend your good taste when I say that they were cheap fabrics put together with inferior workmanship in styles that have not been in vogue for more than two years. Miss Bridges, although not quite up to the standards of the top London houses, has excellent taste and the best of fabrics, and her workmanship cannot be faulted."

Emmeline looked hurt. "You were ashamed of me," she accused.

"Never, my love," he reassured her. "Your beauty would shine through any garment you wore."

She looked at him suspicously. "You're funning, aren't you? Even Papa never said I was beautiful."

"I wouldn't tease you, my dear. Not on something so important to you. At sixteen you were probably a lanky schoolgirl, all legs and arms that you didn't quite know what to do with." She looked at him in surprise and emphatically nodded her agreement. "But in the two years since then, you have rounded out very nicely, and you now have the kind of good looks that last. You may be wrinkled, but you'll still be beautiful at eighty. Wait until you see my grandmama, and you'll know just what I mean."

She smiled a little shyly at him. "Thank you for telling me that, Charles."

"Thank me properly," he growled, and sat back, waiting.

A little hesitantly, she put her arms around his neck, her fingers starting to play with the black curling tendrils of his hair. As she looked into them, the dark pools of his gray eyes twinkled just a little and made her feel as though she was drowning in them. She brought her lips close to his gently smiling mouth, and as they lightly touched, his lips ignited fires through hers in a blazing path to the innermost parts of her body.

His arms enfolded her as he took possession of her entire mouth, and through it every inch of her body. When at last their lips parted, they were both completely shaken by the depth of their feelings and for once even Charles was speechless. Emmeline remained in his arms, her face buried in his chest, until she was back to something like her usual self.

"I think we'd better save that for our bedchamber in the future," he said ruefully. "Can you believe that I wanted to take my own wife right here on the riverbank?"

Eleven

Emmeline was overcome by the amplitude of her wardrobe. It was at least four times that of her mother's and sister's wardrobes combined—and, as Charles had pronounced, these were just clothes for traveling and staying with his family. When she reached London she would be making even more fashionable purchases.

As Betty carefully packed the evening gowns, Emmeline could hear her murmur in awe at the beauty of each. There was a gown of sea-green gauze over a white satin slip, with its bodice and tiny puff sleeves trimmed with seed pearls and white lace; one of sapphire blue silk, with a deep round neckline, tiny sleeves, and a sash of gold velvet tied under the breasts in a bow, the points of which reached almost to the hem; a deep rose silk gown with a silver net overskirt caught up with bows of deep rose velvet, tiny ones at the top, graduating to large ones around the hem; and one very plain, sleeveless column of bronze satin that made her hair look like pure gold.

That the London dressmakers could improve upon these, Emmeline found difficult to conceive.

She had supposed that Betty would travel with them, but Charles had been quite adamant. She must have a most proficient abigail, accustomed to dressing hair in the height of fashion, and experienced enough to ensure that Emmeline always wore the correct garments and accessories for the occasion. To obtain such a person he had enlisted the services of his sister, Margaret, who had at last secured a person with the highest qualifications for the post. The abigail would be at his sister's home when they arrived a few days hence.

Emmeline was not sure who she was the more nervous of meeting, Charles's sister or this unknown paragon of excellence who was to be her abigail.

After what seemed to her an endless period of preparation, but which Charles assured her was excessively speedy for a female, everything was packed, she had personally numbered and listed the contents of each piece of her luggage, and everything was stowed away in the second of the two traveling coaches. This coach would carry, in addition to the luggage, Charles's valet and her abigail, while she and Charles would ride in the newer, more elegant, and very much more comfortable carriage.

In view of the misunderstandings that had happened when he had ridden outside the carriage on their trip from Yorkshire, Charles was determined that this time he would travel inside with Emmeline. She was very young and still unsure of herself, and he had come to realize his obligation to extend his support during her introduction to his family and society. He was becoming increasingly fond of her and was anxious to make her debut as easy as possible.

They left at nine o'clock in the morning, and after a stop for luncheon, it was no more than four hours before they were passing through the gates and down a long entrance road to the elegant mansion which was the country house of Lord and Lady Exeter.

Footmen poured through the wide front door as the carriage came to a halt. Charles alighted first, then turned to help Emmeline down. He felt her tremble by his side as they approached the house, and so squeezed her hand as they climbed the steps and entered the impressive hall.

Emmeline's first glance took in the liveried footmen at each door, then moved upward to see a young woman, very beautiful with a glowing complexion and black hair, and grown quite large with child, coming slowly down the staircase, holding on tightly to the balustrade as she descended.

"Charles, Emmeline, please stay exactly where you are and I'll be with you as soon as I can get down these wretched stairs. Robert has forbidden me to hasten and made me swear to hold on, so it takes me an age to descend." The last words were uttered a trifle breathlessly as she reached the hall.

Brother and sister embraced warmly, then turned to Emmeline, who made a pretty curtsy to her new sister-in-law. Margaret took one look at Emmeline's pale, serious face with the blue eyes dark with worry, and opened her arms to her, giving her as warm an embrace as she had her brother.

"My dear, I'm so happy to be the first to welcome you into our family. Charles has probably warned you that your stay is unlikely to be a quiet one, but I hope it will be most enjoyable, nonetheless."

She turned back to her brother. "Charles, why don't you give any orders you need to about your coaches and cattle, while I take Emmeline up to your chambers. I've already ordered tea and refreshments to be served at once, as I'm sure you must both be sadly in need of sustenance."

With an arm around Emmeline's shoulders, she steered her toward the big staircase and they slowly mounted the stairs while Margaret chattered merrily away. Briefly glancing back at Charles, Emmeline saw his raised eyebrows, helpless shrug, and wide "I told you so" grin.

When they at last reached the huge bedchamber, a serious-looking, middle aged woman in a dark uniform, with gray hair pulled tightly back in a bun, awaited them.

"This is Marianne, who is to be your abigail while you're here, and then if she suits, you may want to make the position a permanent one. She is from France, but speaks excellent English."

Marianne curtsied gravely, and Emmeline smiled briefly in acknowledgment, then reached into her reticule for the listing she had made of the contents of each piece of luggage. "From this enumeration I made, I am sure you will know what to unpack first." She pointed to an entry. "This is the gown I should like to wear tonight."

By her efficient handling of the abigail and her pleasant manner, no one could have guessed her nervousness, but then Emmeline had always gotten along well with the staff at Grantley Range. It was now up to the abigail to prove her efficiency by finding the right accessories for the gown.

After splashing her hands and face from a bowl of water and rose petals, Emmeline removed her bonnet, patted her hair smooth, and followed Margaret into the drawing room.

"You mean to say that you made a complete listing of everything in that mountain of luggage?" Margaret asked admiringly as she seated herself before the tea table and prepared to pour. "How competent you must be! It has never entered my head to do so when we travel, and for days we always have the most awful time trying to find things."

Emmeline flushed with pleasure. "Well, not all of the luggage. I didn't touch his lordship's things. And I will expect my abigail to perform the task in the future," she asserted hastily, not wishing to give the impression she did servants' work.

Margaret was still smiling with delight. "And I will expect my abigail and the children's nanny to list our packing like that in the future, also. You see, I am already indebted to you, Emmeline."

Charles entered with his brother-in-law Robert, and after introductions had been performed they ate delicious biscuits, cakes, and pastries, and sipped China tea. Robert and Margaret were charming hosts, and Emmeline didn't realize how quickly the time had passed until Margaret rose to dress for dinner, explaining that she needed extra time as she always visited the children's nursery at this hour.

Emmeline set down her tea cup. "Would it be too much of an imposition, Margaret, if I came with you?" she asked. "I'm most anxious to meet your children."

Charles groaned. "That's the first mistake you've made, Emmeline," he said, gazing at her with mock horror. "After that long drive the very last thing I want to see are Margaret's monsters."

His sister bristled. "Really, Charles! How can you say such a thing? They can be a little tiring though, Emmeline, so if you are having second thoughts you may wish to put it off till tomorrow."

For answer, Emmeline crossed the room and went out with her. The nursery was on the same floor, but in the other wing, and despite the solid walls, screams and shrieks could still be heard some distance from the door.

The sight of a strange lady momentarily quieted the children. They stood and eyed her suspiciously, and Margaret took advantage of the silence to make the introductions.

"Our first son, Robert III, is just seven years old."

Black haired and looking very much like Charles must have at the same age, the boy made an attempt at a bow. "And our only daughter, Anne, has seen five summers." A rebellious little girl with fiery auburn curls glared as she attempted a curtsy and ended on her bottom on the floor.

"Then Martin is our baby, a two-and-a-half-year-old bundle of mischief, aren't you?" Margaret said lovingly, as she scooped up the angelic fair-haired child.

"Your ladyship, please! He's much too rough and heavy for you now." Nanny looked old enough to have been Charles's and Margaret's own nanny, and as Martin started to jump around and kick in Margaret's arms, she became most alarmed and struggled to take the reluctant child from his mother.

Emmeline decided that the baby was already receiving enough attention from the other two women, and turned to Anne, who had remained sitting on the floor where she tumbled. Perching on the arm of a chair nearby, Emmeline said to no one in particular but loud enough for Anne to hear, "I never liked visitors to the nursery when I was a little girl. We always had to stop our play while they asked stupid questions."

Anne looked at her suspiciously at first, then imperceptibly inched closer. "Did your brother always boss you about, too?" she asked cautiously.

"I didn't have an older brother—it was an older sister—and she used to tell tales about me besides just bossing." Emmeline still didn't look at the little girl, but just talked into space.

Anne was now sitting on the floor below the chair, and carefully she edged up until she sat completely in the chair. A tiny hand stole comfortingly onto Emmeline's lap, and the little girl nodded sagely. "Yes, telling tales is much worse. Robbie doesn't tell tales," she said, suddenly proud of her big brother.

Very lightly, Emmeline covered the little hand with her own, at the same time turning toward her. "I'm sure he doesn't, Anne. Telling tales is awful."

"Can an aunt be a friend?" The solemn face looked up at Emmeline, the frame of copper curls reminding her of a delicate china doll.

"Yes, Anne, and I would be happy to be your friend," Emmeline told her, equally seriously, and the bond was sealed.

As she was leaving, Robert came up to her. "You won't change your mind, will you? Anne needs a woman friend," he said, with all the earnestness of an adult, and Emmeline realized he'd overheard the conversation.

"No, I won't change my mind. I'll always be her friend, Robert," she assured him. His smile was so very much like Charles's that Emmeline wanted to hug him, but knew he'd be embarrassed if she tried.

When they were outside the nursery, Margaret remarked casually, "You know, I'm surprised. I would have thought that your first interest would have been in the baby of the family."

Emmeline laughed. "Between you and Nanny he was getting all the attention. I'll meet him later, but you have two adorable older children, Margaret."

Margaret beamed with pride as they parted at Emmeline's door.

The new abigail was waiting. The chosen dress, a cream-colored muslin trimmed in apricot and gold, had been pressed, and apricot gloves and slippers and a cream and gold fan were placed alongside it. Most welcome, though, was the copper tub filled with steaming, scented water, and Emmeline gladly allowed herself to be undressed and bathed in unaccustomed luxury. She was very tired, and Marianne's hands were most gentle as they patted her dry, then helped her into the necessary undergarments and the lovely new gown.

All this had been accomplished in silence, but finally Marianne spoke. "Avez-vous—you 'ave a special style you wish your hair, your ladyship, or perhaps I try something different?"

"Try it your way, Marianne. I'm too tired to think about it tonight, and mean to retire as early as possible."

Just then Charles came in and heard the last sentence. "If you're so tired, my love, we can make our excuses and have something sent up here. It was a long day of traveling, after all."

"No, I couldn't disappoint your sister, Charles. She's looking forward so very much to seeing us both tonight." She turned around to smile up at him disarmingly. "You'd better sit next to me and give me a poke each time I doze off."

"We'll more likely face each other, and I'll have to kick your shins." He grimaced as he started untying his cravat before going back through the connecting door. "How did you get along with Margaret's brats?"

"I liked them, or at least I liked the older two. The baby was being pulled backward and forward between Margaret and Nanny the whole time, so I talked with Robert and Anne."

Marianne was piling her blond hair high on top of her head as she spoke, and when Emmeline turned back to the mirror, she scarcely recognized the beautiful person reflected there. "Don't go for a minute, Charles," she called before he closed the door. "Tell me what you think of my hair."

He stood behind her and looked at her reflection in the mirror. "It's magnificent, my dear. The gown is lovely also, and you are very beautiful, despite such a wearisome day."

"Oh, this is Marianne, my new abigail." As the girl dropped a curtsy, Charles nodded, then bent over Emmeline to place a kiss on her lips. "I'll be ready in about a half-hour, and will be honored to escort such a lovely lady."

Their visit lasted a week, at the end of which Emmeline had become a great favorite with all the Exeters, parents and children alike.

Marianne was very efficient, unusually quiet, and could work wonders with Emmeline's hair, so it was decided that she should remain as her abigail. She traveled with them, in the second coach with the valet, to the country home of the Marquess and Marchioness of Millford, Charles's father and mother.

Emmeline fell in love with the house and its formal gardens as soon as she saw it through the windows of the carriage. It was, understandably, a much larger and more dignified house than the one they had just left. This time no one came down the wide stairs to allay her fears and welcome them, but Bentley had everything well in hand and they were shown immediately to their bedchambers to rest and refresh themselves before joining her ladyship for tea.

Having been too nervous to eat anything all day, Emmeline now became silently panic-stricken, sure that Charles's parents disapproved of the marriage and were trying to make it clear from the start. To anyone who didn't know her well, she seemed outwardly very calm, but her eyes gave her away, having deepened with fear to a dark blue, and her hands would not keep still unless she held them together.

Dismissing her abigail on the pretext of resting for a while, she lay back in a deep wingchair near the crackling fire and no longer even tried to stop shaking. It was there that Charles found her when he came into the room, and after taking a careful look at her closed eyes and clasped hands, and noting the shivers passing through her, he went purposefully from the chamber.

The marchioness was in her private withdrawing room,

resting in a favorite chair. Her eyes brightened as he entered. "Charles, how lovely to see you alone for a few minutes. Margaret wrote such a nice letter about your bride. It seems they all loved her so much. Is she resting after the journey?"

Charles took her hand in his and bent to kiss her cheek.

"First, Mama, how is Father?"

"Much better, I'm thankful to say. He's greatly improved, heeding the doctor's advice for once, and I know he'll be even better for seeing you. He's also looking forward to meeting Emmeline." She looked quizzically at him. "Is everything all right?"

"No, Mama, everything's not all right. Emmeline is only eighteen, you know, and she's determined to become the good wife she thinks I deserve." He smiled at the recollection of her earnestness. "She was in a panic at the thought of meeting Margaret, but as we arrived my dear sister came down the stairs to greet us warmly, and they were immediately the best of friends.

"She hasn't eaten anything today, Mama, and scarcely spoke a word during the drive until she saw the house and couldn't help falling in love with it. Right now she's sitting in her bedchamber, eyes closed, white knuckled, and I could actually see her trembling. She's terrified at the prospect of meeting you, sure that you won't like her." He looked at her appealingly. "Will you . . . ?"

She interrupted him with a wave of her hand as she rose. "How insensitive of me! It's been thirty years, but I'd never have believed I could forget my fear and trepidation when I was to meet your grandmama for the first time." She was already at the door. "It's best that I see her alone. Go and pay your respects to your father."

EMMELINE DIDN'T HEAR the door close, but there must have been some sound, for she opened her eyes to see a most beautiful older lady standing by her chair. She tried to rise and curtsy, but a gentle hand detained her.

"Don't get up, my dear. Charles is with his father, and I came to get to know you. I had the loveliest letter from Margaret, singing your praises to the heavens, but she didn't tell me how exquisite you are."

"My lady . . ." Emmeline began, but a raised hand again stopped her.

"Let me just get settled, and I'll tell you a story," the marchioness said, easing herself into the opposite chair. "Charles's father was visiting in the part of Devon where I lived when we met. It was a whirlwind courtship, for we knew from the start we were meant for each other and must wed. He spoke to my father, then he took me to meet his family. I had never met a marchioness. In fact, though I was the daughter of a baron, I was still a country girl at heart. Emmeline, I was terrified! They were very formal people and to this day I have never really been able to relax with them the way I hope you will with the marquess and me."

She rose, holding out both hands to her lovely new daughter-in-law. "Will you forgive me, Emmeline, for forgetting how it feels, and allow me to welcome you to our home as our second daughter?" Her hazel eyes wreathed by fine wrinkles yet still beautiful, reflected the warmth of her welcoming smile.

A little sheepishly, Emmeline took her hands and submitted to the older woman's embrace.

"Thank you. I've never met a marchioness before either, and I didn't know what to expect," she explained. "Did Charles ask you to come?"

"Not in so many words, my dear. He described your feelings and thus reminded me of the time when I'd been in the same predicament." Her eyes twinkled mischievously. "You do realize, don't you, that you will be the Marchioness of Millford one day?"

"Oh, dear. I hadn't thought of that." Emmeline's eyes were wide with surprise. "But I hope that it won't be for a very long time."

The marchioness nodded in agreement. "Now we'd better decide what you are to call me. Would your mother object if you also called me Mama? You could differentiate, when necessary, with Mama Millford and Mama—Barrow?"

"Grantley," Emmeline said decidedly, then remembering herself, added, "I beg your pardon, Mama. I forgot to ask after Lord Millford. I hope his condition has improved."

"I'm happy to say that he's much better. I believe the news of Charles's marriage did much to help. And when he sees you, my dear, he will be enchanted, I know." She paused, considering how to phrase the next question. "Although not going into any detail, Charles gave me to understand that you were not very happy at home. Is your stepfather a problem?"

"I was very happy when my father was alive. I think we all were, but Lord Barrow despises me. Please don't let us talk about him." Emmeline was not yet adept at changing from an unpleasant subject. "Charles said that his grandmama would be the only one in London for the Season. Will she have to sponsor me?"

"Yes, she'll present you at court, give a ball for you, get you vouchers for Almack's, and things like that. Don't worry about the work. She may grumble, but she'll enjoy herself, and she has lots of help. But you'll have to behave yourself, as she won't tolerate any deviation from what is accepted by the *haut ton*. When she says you must do something, she'll expect to be obeyed," Lady Millford warned ruefully. "No outings without a maid, no riding without a groom in attendance, and so forth. It's considerably different from being in the country."

"She sounds rather like Lady Poole, whom I've grown to like very much," Emmeline observed unthinkingly.

"She is like Lady Poole, but I wasn't aware that you knew her. They're very old friends, and keep in close touch," Lady Millford advised. "Of course. Poole House is quite close to Charles's home in Warwickshire so naturally you have met."

Emmeline hid a sigh of relief. She had better be careful what she said about Lady Poole in the future. She'd find it difficult to explain to the marchioness why she had been so foolish as to run away from her son.

It was by now time for tea, and they went together to the empty drawing room. Bentley was instructed to request the gentlemen to join the ladies for refreshments, and they arrived at the same time as the tea tray.

The marquess held Emmeline's hand for a long time, seeing her father clearly in her features and coloring, and then the two of them sat in a corner of the room, getting to know each other and swapping stories about Lord Grantley. When tea was over she felt as if she'd known this big, kind gentleman all of her life.

IT HAD BEEN a most successful day and, tired but happy, Emmeline dismissed Marianne and waited, hoping that Charles would join her. She was not disappointed. Within five minutes he entered the bedchamber in a deep green silk dressing gown.

"Feeling better than you did this morning, my love?" he asked, as he tenderly stroked her ear and the delicate curve of her jaw.

"Very much better, thanks to you. They couldn't be nicer. You were so patient with me . . ."

He silenced her with a deep kiss that left her breathless and with no desire to waste further time in talk. It was still a wonder to her that he could make her body respond to his slightest touch until she wanted him as badly as he wanted her. Greater still was the realization that her hands had so much power over him, and she delighted in watching his excitement build under her caressing fingers.

As they lay relaxing afterward, she remembered her conversation with his mother. "Did you know that Lady Poole is a great friend of your grandmama?" Her voice was a breathless whisper that stirred the damp hairs on his chest where her head rested.

"I'm sure I've heard that she is, but what . . . ? Oh dear, I see what you mean." He winced. "It would seem that we will have to take Grandmama into our confidence when we get to town, and have her hush her friend. Don't worry about it, my love. They're both very experienced and have concealed much worse scandals than that in their time."

During the days that followed, in order to avoid as many problems as possible for Emmeline when she arrived in London, the marchioness went over a great number of do's and don'ts of the *haut ton*, and even instructed her on how to behave when presented at court.

"I don't want Grandmama to find you completely without polish, Emmeline. And you'll be so busy when you get to town, selecting a new wardrobe and then attending all the balls and such," Lady Millford explained.

Once again, Charles and Emmeline were sorry to leave, but made the promise to come back soon for a rest and change of pace, as London was only a half-day's journey away from the Millford estate.

Now all Emmeline had to worry about was Charles's grandmama, who the nicest people said was a dragon, while others said far worse things about her.

Twelve

By the time the carriage drew into Berkeley Square, Emmeline was travel-weary once more. The Millford's London townhouse was large, with six windows either side of a plain gray stone portico and simple pediment. A graveled courtyard set the house back from the street. Glimmering lights could be seen in several of the windows and the flambeaux were lit on either side of the door.

"I believe the Dowager Lady Millford must already be in residence," Charles remarked as he assisted Emmeline from the carriage and up the stone steps of the portico. He immediately regretted his remark as he heard her nervous little gasp. "She may growl fiercely, but if you mention Lady Poole's name she'll eat out of your hand, I'll warrant," he quickly reassured her.

In anticipation of their arrival, the huge knocker had been replaced on the door, and his loud bangs brought an answer within a few minutes. A dignified, white-haired, bewhiskered butler appeared at the door.

As he stepped aside to allow their passage into the great hall, a loud female voice emanated from the head of the magnificent staircase. "Manning, who's calling at this late hour? I'm not yet in residence, d'ye hear?"

"Good evening, Grandmama. Don't come down," Charles called back. "We'll be with you directly."

His hand was like a vise on Emmeline's elbow as he steered her across the marble floor and up the stairs to a gold drawing room. Inside, a fire blazed in the hearth, and a ramrod-spined lady stood as though to attention, awaiting their arrival. Three score and fifteen years had turned her skin to a pale translucence and her hair to a fine, silvery white halo. Fine wrinkles traced a feathery pattern at the corners of her mouth and her watery blue eyes, but her former beauty was still apparent, and the inherent dignity of a marchioness was evidenced in every line.

Charles crossed the room and kissed her cheek. "Grandmama, may I present my bride, Lady Emmeline."

Emmeline swept her a deep curtsy, and the dowager said gruffly, "Come here, child. Let me take a look at you."

In appearance she was nothing like Lady Poole, but her manner was so similar that Emmeline felt little of the nervousness she'd experienced when meeting the other members of Charles's family. She came closer to the marchioness, who looked her critically up and down, then exclaimed, "You really are a child at that! How old are you, missy?"

"I'm turned eighteen, my lady," she replied, a little defiantly.

"That's good. I was the same age when I wed. You should be able to sire a passel of good-looking youngsters now, grandson. She's got the looks. Does she have the breeding?" the old lady demanded.

Feeling somewhat like a brood mare being checked for pedigree, Emmeline bristled, and Charles caught her look. "I'm quite sure Mama has already advised you on that score. Stop trying to bully her, Grandmama. We're both weary and in need of a meal before retiring for the night. We've much to discuss, but nothing that won't hold till the morrow."

He took Emmeline's hand. "Come, my dear. Bid Grandmama a good night and we'll retire to our chambers. I'll arrange for a light repast to be served there shortly."

The dowager raised her cheek for his kiss, then turned to Emmeline. "You're part of the Millford family now, granddaughter." She turned her cheek and Emmeline touched her lips to the cool skin. "Good night, Grandmama," she murmured, taking Charles's hand once more, and together they followed the footman who showed them to their chambers.

Emmeline's was a lovely pale blue bedchamber with an ornate four-poster bed. The window and bed draperies were the palest blue, with pink and cream roses spilling over them, and the same fabric covered the chairs and chaise. Just inside the door she slipped off the shoes she had traveled in, lest they stain the delicate cream carpet, then saw that Marianne was busy in the dressing room unpacking and putting away her clothes.

"Help me undress and bathe, Marianne, then you may leave the rest of the unpacking for morning. You must be as tired as I am, and sorely in need of a good night's sleep." In the past few weeks, she had grown to appreciate her hardworking abigail.

She was still soaking in the copper tub when she felt a roughness in the hands that were washing her and turned to find that Charles had dismissed the maid and was enjoying performing her duties. She stepped out, and he took the large towels and patted her dry, taking great care to get into all the more sensitive places, until she would willingly have forgone the food that awaited them for a more sensual satisfaction.

Charles had more patience, though, and clad in dressing gowns, they entered the sitting room between their two chambers, where a simple meal had been left for them to serve themselves.

Tired as she was, Emmeline yet enjoyed the companionable meal eaten by the light of the one candle and the flames which leaped fiercely about the logs in the tiled fireplace. She felt almost too weary to make conversation, and in fact they spoke little until the last crumb of fruit pie had been eaten.

"You're becoming accustomed to meeting new members of my family, Emmie," Charles remarked, taking a sip from the glass of port that had been brought up with Emmeline's tea tray. "Most people quake before Grandmama's blunt choice of words."

Emmeline smiled. "I liked her. She reminded me so much of Lady Poole, as your mama said she would."

"It would seem your month away was valuable training for dealing with cantankerous old ladies," he said with a low chuckle. "I've always dealt well with Grandmama, but to this day I believe she intimidates Mama."

Her eyelids felt so heavy that Emmeline was having much difficulty keeping them open and, had she been alone, she would have fallen asleep immediately she got into bed. But as Charles drew her away from the table and into his arms, his familiar hands caused her skin to tingle as they first removed her wrapper and then, after unfastening the ribbons of her gown, roved gently around her breasts, making her body spring to life. A low moan escaped her.

She was conscious of his strength as he carried her to her bed, laid her down, then slipped in by her side, pulling the covers over them both. Their loving was gentle, softly delicious as they unerringly found each other's secret places and let their pleasure build slowly until it reached a new crescendo. As their passion lessened its violence and their heartbeats returned to normal, they lay peacefully in each other's arms. He had loved her in a number of different beds in these last weeks, and no matter the setting, each time had been like a comforting, magical dream. She closed her eyes, hugging the thought to her as she fell asleep.

WHEN SHE AWOKE the following morning, Charles was already gone, and she realized it must be quite late. She could hear a much happier Marianne in her dressing room, softly humming a popular French tune, and as the bed creaked the abigail came into the room.

Within a few minutes she was sitting up sipping hot chocolate. Having ascertained that Charles had already breakfasted and was out riding, she agreed to have breakfast in her chamber, as Lady Millford never left hers before noontime. Emmeline spent a lazy morning, not descending to the lower floor until almost twelve o'clock. Finding herself alone, she asked to be shown the library and spent a delightful hour familiarizing herself with books she'd read before, and ones she'd always wanted to read. She realized she would never want for reading material while in London, unless she sought something lighter such as one of Mrs. Radcliffe's latest romances.

She was still selecting a suitable volume when a footman knocked on the door with a request from Lady Millford that she join her in the drawing room. As Emmeline rose from her curtsy, the older lady carefully appraised her, then nodded with a look of satisfaction. "That's better. You look well rested after your journey, Emmeline. Are you going to make my grandson a good wife?"

Emmeline met the demanding look of the older woman. "I am already making him a good wife, my lady," she replied firmly, wishing that Charles had been here for this first meeting. They had decided that his grandmother had to know everything, and Emmeline did not want to be the one to tell her alone.

"You are already a favorite of my good friend, Lady Poole," her ladyship continued, to Emmeline's horror. "She wrote to me briefly and said she was sure you and Charles would explain the unusual circumstances of your meeting with her and, I must admit, I am most curious."

Lady Millford was obviously waiting for an explanation, and Emmeline prayed that Charles would walk in at any moment. "It's a long story, Grandmama. I'm sure you'd prefer to wait until after lunch when Charles and I together can tell you the whole," she murmured as the butler came to announce lunch.

It was with considerable relief that she found Charles awaiting them in the dining room, and after a brief exchange regarding the weather and the paucity of familiar faces in the city this early in the Season, a silence fell over the table while they nibbled on the excellent partridge pie.

When the final course had been removed, the servants left for other duties. Lady Millford presided over the tea tray, taking advantage of the privacy to broach the subject of Lady Poole once more.

"Emmeline has already put me off once, Charles. I now await with considerable impatience the story of your acquaintanceship with my friend, Lady Poole. And don't tell me she is a neighbor of yours in the country, as I have been aware of that detail ever since you came into your inheritance."

There was an edge to her voice, and Emmeline looked questioningly at Charles.

He sighed, then commenced in the most diplomatic way he knew to put Lady Millford in a receptive frame of mind. "This is very confidential, Grandmama. I deemed it best not to inform my dear mama and papa of this matter, but felt you must know everything in order to present Emmeline to society in the best possible way."

Lady Millford cleared her throat loudly, and grunted, "You'd better tell me all and I'll be the judge of that."

Putting Emmeline in a far better light than himself, Charles gave her the gist of the wedding, Emmeline's running away, and his search for and final recovery of his bride.

The old lady listened, then turned to Emmeline. "Do you have anything to add to the story, young lady?"

"Yes, ma'am, I do," she said firmly. "I was at fault, not Charles. I had no right to run away, and was very lucky that I met Lady Poole, and that Charles found me before I ruined my life completely."

"Well, as to that, I doubt that Caroline would have allowed you to continue to London alone. It would seem she became fond of you even before she knew who you were. But how many people may recognize you as her companion?"

"Very few, Grandmama. I wore dark clothes, pulled my hair tightly back in a bun, and used a different name. Lady Poole's cousin would know me, of course, but I'm sure her ladyship has handled that." Emmeline tried to remember which of Lady Poole's guests might come to London for the Season. "There was just one woman who was not very pleasant to me, and was bringing out her two granddaughters this Season. Do you remember her name, Charles? We glimpsed her on the street one day, and I asked that you not stop."

"Oh, I'd forgotten about her," he said, shaking his head. "I'm afraid it was Lady Davenport, Grandmama. And she must have taken a close look at Emmeline. She did her teacup trick over Emmeline's lap because she was so much better looking than her own girls."

"Lady Poole told her that I was the granddaughter of one of her former beaus, if that helps," added Emmeline, "but I was wearing my wedding band and people generally thought me a widow."

Lady Millford appeared to be concentrating on a corner of the tablecloth, grunting occasionally, her lips compressed sternly. Seeing her obvious quandary, Emmeline looked appealingly at Charles, and he gave her a reassuring smile.

When the old lady finally looked up she showed Emmeline a cold, disdainful countenance. "I believe we can pull it off successfully. But you will have to do exactly what I tell you to do, and I will brook no argument. My grandson is enamored and willing to let you get away with anything, but I will not, and at the first sign of rebellion I will wash my hands of the whole matter. Do I make myself understood?" Lady Millford's tone was harsh and she looked at her grandson's wife with distaste.

Emmeline was very disappointed. She had not been in awe of the dowager because of her resemblance to Lady Poole, but now it seemed that in order to gain acceptance by the *haut ton* she would have to put herself in the hands of a dictatorial termagant, and suddenly it did not seem worthwhile.

Charles had remained silent during Lady Millford's ultimatum, and now Emmeline looked toward him and, close to tears, she slowly shook her head before turning back to her ladyship.

"Thank you, ma'am, for being willing to try, but I believe this to be too much of an imposition," she said very quietly. "I am a country girl and cannot guarantee to always live up to your high standards. I believe that, under the circumstances, it would be better for Charles to return me to Warwickshire where he can join me after he has had his fill of the Season's delights."

She got up and started toward the door, but Charles caught her hand and drew her toward him.

"Come, Emmeline, where's my young bride who was so excited at being part of the Season, getting tickets for Almack's, and attending balls?" he asked, gently teasing.

But Emmeline was too upset. She felt that she'd been tried and found guilty by his grandmother, and all she wished was to hide herself in the country and hope that Charles would join her there. She pulled herself out of his arms and almost ran out of the room.

Lady Millford gazed after her, a frown on her face. "Is she always so impulsive, Charles? I take it that this is an act intended for my benefit so that I will allow her more latitude, but she's mistaken. I meant what I said about her behavior."

Charles was irritated with both Emmeline and Lady Millford. He knew that Emmeline meant every word she said. His grandmother's disapproval had been the last straw, and she just wanted to go home.

"There is one thing you should know about Emmeline, Grandmama. She doesn't put on acts, in fact she is just about the most open creature I've ever met. I can promise you that at this moment her abigail has started packing." He gave her ladyship a rueful grin. "If it's what she really wishes, she shall return to the country, but I will accompany and stay with her, as it seems I have no desire to be with anyone else. Perhaps in a year or so, when society has become used to our marriage and Mama is in a position to introduce her, we will come back for a Season."

Before he finished speaking, Lady Millford pushed herself to her feet and glared at her grandson belligerently. "I suppose you want me to go up to her and beg her to stay? Tell her she may do as she likes and I'll cover for her, or some such thing?" she asked with a snort.

"No, Grandmama, that is not what I want, and I cannot remember the last time you begged for anything, nor can you, I'm sure." He walked toward the door, holding it for her to pass ahead of him. "I feel you two should get to know each other before any decisions are made. I suppose it would be beneath your dignity to go to her bedchamber and talk to her?" he remarked with some asperity.

"You watch your manners, young man," her ladyship said wrathfully. "You're not yet too old for me to box your ears, you know."

Charles chuckled. "A little too tall, though. You'd have to insist that I sit down first." He placed an affectionate arm around her rigid shoulders. "Your friend holds her in the highest regard. Why don't you give yourself a chance to get to know her properly before you start to bully her?"

With a sniff, Lady Millford started toward the staircase, and Charles pretended an interest in the card tray until he saw her turn in the direction of Emmeline's room.

AN UNHAPPY MARIANNE, who had just finished unpacking for her mistress, was busily packing everything again while Emmeline sat looking into the fire, watching the flames leap up the back of the fireplace, then fizzle back down into the coals. She had taken little heed of Charles's mother when she told her that she had always been in awe of Lady Millford. How foolish she had been to think that because Lady Poole liked her, her friend would also! But there had been no mistaking the look of contempt on her ladyship's face when she had consented to present her, "under certain conditions."

When the knock sounded on her door, Emmeline supposed it was Charles, but was surprised he would knock. Marianne opened the door and had to step back quickly as Lady Millford swept past her into the chamber. Seating herself opposite Emmeline, she came straight to the point. "My grandson has suggested that before any decisions are made, you and I should get to know each other," she said abruptly. "And I think it's a very good idea."

Marianne looked up from her packing, and Emmeline dismissed her with a nod. Then she turned back to the dowager. "My lady, it is my belief that when Charles and I have been married a few years, and we've made a start on the passsel of youngsters you spoke about, your opinion of me may improve, but there is nothing I can tell you that will make you change that opinion right now."

"Stop being so hoity-toity with me, girl! I've come to try to make friends with you. The least you can do is meet me halfway," the old lady snapped.

Lady Millford was glaring so at her that Emmeline's sense of humor came to the fore, and she had to laugh. "Pardon me, ma'am, but no one ever tried to make friends with me wearing such a glower," she said, then impulsively reached for her ladyship's hand. "Please don't feel you have to do this, Grandmama. I promise I would never try to alienate Charles from any of his family no matter how you feel about me," she assured her earnestly.

The old lady looked down at the smooth white hand holding her wrinkled one, then up at Emmeline's sincere face. "I think you'd better tell me a little about yourself, starting with how you and Charles met," she said gruffly, and cleared her throat.

That action instantly reminded Emmeline of Lady Poole. The latter had always become brusque and cleared her throat when she felt emotional, and Emmeline had been too full of her own thoughts to recognize the similarity between the two old friends.

She'd never had the opportunity to tell Lady Poole all about herself, so now she pretended to be talking to her instead of to her friend, and her nervousness vanished as she told her story simply, with little emotion except insofar as it affected Charles. When she spoke of him, her voice grew husky and she unwittingly told Lady Millford more than she realized herself about her feelings for her husband.

By the time she was finished, it was Lady Millford who was holding Emmeline's hand, and patting it gently.

"You've done a few foolish things, my dear, but nothing that is of account to anyone except you and Charles," she said finally. "I remember making a number of much more foolish mistakes than yours when I was first married, and I didn't have a husband as kind and understanding as Charles, but I had plenty of nerve, and I held up my head and brazened them through. And I'll do it again for you, if need be."

Emmeline had started to shake her head, but the old lady stopped her with an upraised hand.

"Talk it over with Charles before you go any further with that packing," she advised. "I was harsh with you downstairs, I know, and I can't promise I'll not be so again, but I'll try not to be, and you can hold me to it." She smiled dreamily and her eyes acquired a sparkle. "Y'know, it would be fun to get back into society once again. I haven't been among young people for the longest time, and I'm beginning to look forward to it."

She kissed Emmeline on the cheek and took her leave to have her afternoon nap, making her promise to reconsider her decision.

When she'd gone, Emmeline sat for a while, thinking how it might be to enter society with the old lady firmly behind her and Charles at her side. The decision wasn't a difficult one, and didn't need Charles's persuasion. Anticipating Marianne's disapproval, she emptied the portmanteau and started to put her clothes back into the wardrobe.

"Are you reverting to your former duties, Emmie, or is your abigail indisposed?"

Charles moved very quietly for a large man. Emmeline gave a start at the sound of his voice, then shook out the garment she had just taken from the bed and put it away. He watched her from the entrance to her bedchamber, eyebrows lifted indolently, a slight smile on his face.

"Am I to assume that her ladyship convinced you to stay and face the *beau monde* together?" he asked, his smile broadening to a grin.

Emmeline couldn't help feeling a little ashamed of her outburst downstairs, sure that Charles had been instrumental in persuading the older lady to talk once more with her. She flushed slightly, and looked up into his face.

"I owe you an apology for my poor manners, sir," she said, feeling wretched. "I trust you will forget my remarks about sending me to the country."

He reached out to draw her into his arms and rested his cheek against her soft hair. "I thought it might come to blows at first, but you handled her very well. Unfortunately, she thought you were bluffing, and I found it necessary to enlighten her."

He dropped a kiss on the tip of her nose, and she raised her head to give him her lips, reveling in the tingling that started there and spread through the rest of her body.

It was with obvious reluctance that Charles relaxed his hold on her and released her lips. "I came up to tell you that if all was well, I had planned to take you driving in the Park this afternoon. Would you like that, my love?"

She smiled a little shyly. "I would be delighted, my lord. It would take only a moment for me to get ready."

"Let's make it fifteen minutes, and Marianne can

help you. We should not meet many people so early in the Season, but one can never tell." He dropped a kiss on her forehead, rang for her abigail, and left the chamber.

It was an excited Emmeline who listened patiently to her abigail's lecture, the closest thing Marianne had yet come to giving her a scold, on what the well-dressed young matron wore for a carriage ride in the Park. With her face and lips still rosy from Charles's attention, she made a glowing picture as she descended the stairs and was helped into the waiting carriage for her very first outing in London.

Thirteen

Charles had already returned from a brisk ride in the Park and was halfway through a substantial breakfast by the time Emmeline had dressed and entered the dining room. She had once more argued with Marianne as to what she should wear and had finally bowed to the abigail's better judgment, although she still considered it completely unnecessary to waste so much time on her appearance.

She was still in a somewhat rebellious frame of mind as she greeted her husband and told the footman what she would like. Charles, by now well able to read her face, gave her a curious glance. Once the footman had left the room, she took a deep breath, prepared to tell him what she thought of London ways. But with an apologetic grin, he forestalled her by telling her that her morning was to be spent with him at one of the most exclusive dressmakers and milliners in town.

"You mean that you will actually enter the dressmaker's establishment, Charles? Is this customary?" She felt compelled to ask him, knowing that neither her father nor her stepfather had taken any part in the selection of her mother's gowns.

"Quite customary, my dear," he said with a teasing little smile. "However, it is not usual for a gentleman to assist in the selection of gloves, reticules, and such. For this purpose I have prevailed upon the sister of a very good friend of mine, Sir David Graham, to accompany us to Madame Rolande's and later to help you in selecting the other items you will need."

"Is that really necessary?" she protested. "Surely Marianne could come with me—" she started to say, but he interrupted her.

"Marianne is not a lady of fashion," he said firmly. "Ariadne has exquisite taste, as you will quickly realize, and I believe you will enjoy her company." He chuckled. "You have yet to learn the pleasures of shopping, Emmie, and I'm sure you'll find your initiation most enjoyable."

She realized he was trying to please her, as well as provide her with a guide through the labyrinth of society's fashions, fads, and taboos. She only hoped that Ariadne was not some starchy matron who would treat her like a foolish girl.

It was a very pleasant surprise therefore to find that Lady Ariadne Graham was a very lovely young woman, just three years her senior, who was overjoyed at the prospect of helping Emmeline through these first difficult weeks in the city. Her bonnet of sea blue revealed hair as black as a raven's wing, and with Emmeline's silver-blond hair, the two young women were perfect foils for each other.

Charles was well-known to the dressmaker, and Emmeline couldn't help but speculate on the identities of the other ladies on whom he had spent time and money choosing costly creations, for it was soon obvious that this was the most fashonable mantua-maker in London.

After assisting in the selection of more than twenty garments—walking dresses, morning dresses, redingotes, pelisses, and ball gowns—Charles left the two ladies to their own devices while he went to one of his clubs. Emmeline had swatches of the fabrics they had selected, and Ariadne took her to the Pantheon Bazaar to look for matching reticules, parasols, gloves, shawls, and trinkets. After they had visited several establishments, the footman was loaded with parcels and Emmeline, new to the extravagances of London shopping, could no longer count how much she had spent or charged to Charles's account.

Lady Ariadne then took Emmeline to one of the fashionable tearooms and they lingered over tea and cakes until there was only just time to return to Berkeley Square and change for a drive in the Park. Charles was waiting, and Marianne had a pretty apple-green gown freshly ironed and ready for her to wear.

"I don't know from whom you learned your promptness, Emmie," Charles remarked when they were out of the traffic and entering the Park through the Stanhope Gate, "but it is such a pleasure not to be kept waiting. I hope that a London Season will not serve to make you forget such a delightfully unfeminine trait."

She shook her head, a smile tugging at the corners of her mouth. "I wouldn't dare keep you waiting, my lord," she said gravely.

He looked so very handsome as he gave her an answering grin that she felt the other women in the many barouches, tilburies, and curricles must be envying her. Heads turned in their direction and many passersby bowed or smiled, in greeting, but Charles, while acknowledging them, made no move to stop for conversation. He had really only come out for the airing and did not want to introduce Emmeline to society until she could be seen at her very best.

IT WAS FORTUNATE that by the evening when Almack's opened for the Season, Emmeline had received several of her new gowns. She and Marianne selected one of moss green gauze over white satin, with rosettes and ribbons of white velvet trimming the front and hem, to wear to the opening ball.

Charles looked in just before she finished dressing, and a few minutes later he returned with a magnificent pearl necklace. He placed it in her hand for her examination and she was amazed to find that the emerald clasp had her initials set in diamonds.

He took it from her and fastened it around her neck, and she knew it to be the finest piece of jewelry she had ever owned. "What would have happened had I worn the blue gown, Charles?" she asked teasingly.

He appeared to consider for a moment. "You'll find out when you wear it, minx," he told her, grinning at her reflection in the mirror.

Her brow wrinkled as she tried to recall all that she'd heard about Almack's. "Did you think to secure a voucher for me, my lord?"

"Of course, my dear. Grandmama took care of that some time ago," he assured her. "But I will have to take you to one of the hostesses to secure permission for you to waltz."

She made a face at him, and allowed Marianne to continue dressing her hair. When she was as perfect as her abigail could make her, she drew on long white gloves of softest French kid, and allowed Charles to lead her downstairs and into the waiting carriage.

Charles looked very dashing in his black velvet coat, breeches, white hose, and black shoes. His white neckcloth was starched and tied to perfection, and folded and tucked under his arm was the tricorn hat which he had assured her earlier was *de rigueur*.

She tried hard to conceal her excitement at finally entering the Assembly Rooms. Her first impression was that the company glittered every bit as brightly as did the enormous crystal chandeliers. She made her curtsy to two of the Lady Patronesses, Lady Sally Jersey, who had provided her voucher, and the charming Lady Sefton. Then Charles, having secured their permission, swung her into a waltz.

Emmeline had been unaccustomed to formal dancing, except at the few local balls in the north which she had attended after her family was out of mourning. But she had watched closely when Agatha, just seventeen, had had a dancing master to teach her the various country dances. She hadn't dared let her mother see how much she loved to dance, so she would hide in a corner of the old ballroom at Grantley Range while her sister received instruction, and would try to memorize the steps. Then when they had left and she had the room completely to herself, she would hum the tunes and, after curtsying to her imaginary partner, float gracefully around the floor.

The waltz was a dance she had only heard spoken about as being very daring, but Grandmama Millford had hired the services of a dance teacher for several afternoons, so that she felt completely assured now, as she was swept around the floor in the arms of the most handsome man in the room. Instinctively she was aware of many pairs of eyes watching them as they spun and dipped, and knew they must make a striking couple.

"You dance very well, Emmie. Where did you learn to dance like this?" Charles asked, with an admiring glance at his wife. Her cheeks were a little flushed with the exertion, her eyes sparkled, and her soft lips were parted slightly with excitement.

"Grandmama hired a teacher for me so that I wouldn't embarrass you, my lord," she told him, pleased at the unexpected compliment.

When the music ended, she was quite breathless. Charles led her toward a group of people, the only one she recognized being Ariadne. Introductions were made and Sir David Graham, Ariadne's brother, immediately asked her for the next dance, which was a cotillion with which she was familiar.

It seemed that Charles had a great many friends, and all of them wanted to dance with Emmeline, so that her card quickly became filled, and she could recall very few names of the many young men she had danced with before she realized that Charles was no longer among the group.

Ariadne noticed her looking around and guessed the cause. "Are you worrying about Charles, Emmeline?" she asked. "You know it is not at all the thing to dance more than once with your spouse. I'll venture to guess your card is already filled, isn't it?"

Emmeline looked embarrassed. "Yes it is, but I thought he might stay close just this first time. I don't see him anywhere."

"Oh, he probably met some crony of his and is sitting in one of the salons discussing the news from Aix-la-Chapelle, or the latest extravagances of the Prince Regent." Ariadne could see nothing unusual in this.

Emmeline was still concerned about his absence, however, and was much relieved to see him crossing the floor toward the group as her partner returned her to them after the next dance. Another waltz was about to commence and Lord Peter Fogarty, a blond-haired young man introduced to Emmeline by Ariadne, was to be her partner. Just as he was about to take her hand, however, Charles appeared by her side.

"Sorry, Peter, I'm claiming a husband's special privilege for all waltzes," he told his friend with a smile. "Perhaps Lady Emmeline has a cotillion free later."

The young man looked a little put out, but accepted his lot with good grace, and Charles swept Emmeline onto the floor once more.

"I was hoping to dance with you again, Charles, but

that was very poorly done, don't you think?" she scolded lightly. "He seemed such a pleasant young man, too."

"Don't be concerned, my dear. Peter won't mind too much, but perhaps next time I'd better mark your card and there will be no hurt feelings. I hadn't realized you were going to be so very popular," he teased.

It was heavenly to glide around the floor with his arm around her waist. The flesh beneath his fingers felt as if it were on fire, though his hold was quite light, and her body started to ache with need for him. Emmeline didn't want further discussion. It might not be fashionable to dance with one's husband, but he was the only man in the room she really wanted to be with. She was so surprised and sorry when the dance ended that she failed to conceal her disappointment.

"Smile, my love," Charles advised kindly. "You look as though I trod all over your toes. Perhaps I was wrong and you'd rather I not steal all the waltzes?"

She shook her head and managed a weak smile. "Please, Charles, it was so delightful I didn't want it to end." She could hardly tell him that he had made her long to go home and to bed with him.

But it seemed he had much the same idea. "I know it's your first ball, and you'll probably want to dance until dawn," he said ruefully, "but if you should become tired, please do not hesitate to let me know. It would be my pleasure to take you home."

She could not resist the look in his eyes. "After the next two dances?" she suggested.

He looked very smug as he nodded and handed her back to Ariadne and his friends.

Twenty minutes later, they entered their waiting carriage, and as it started to carry them through the dark quiet streets, Emmeline asked the question uppermost in her mind since he had suggested leaving.

"What excuse did you give for our going home so

early in the evening, my lord? Surely they must have been curious?" she asked.

"Not at all. I didn't tell them we were going home but implied that we had a couple of other affairs to go to. Then if Ariadne or anyone asks later, all you need tell them is that you suddenly felt tired and decided to go home instead." He sounded very pleased with himself as he drew her toward him and let her head rest comfortably on his shoulder.

In the large hall Charles paused for a moment. "Would you care to join me in the library for a brandy?" he suggested.

Emmeline was puzzled. Then she remembered that no alcohol was served at Almack's and presumed this to be the reason for his invitation. "I'd like to join you, but I don't believe I would care for brandy," she started to say as his arm went around her shoulders and he ushered her into the library.

Despite her protest Charles poured two glasses of the amber liquid and handed one to her. "Sip it," he instructed.

The drink burned a fiery trail from her throat deep inside her, and if she didn't quite enjoy it, she didn't at all mind the warm feeling it left in its wake.

Charles was standing with his back to the fireplace, leaning against the mantel, brandy glass in hand, facing Emmeline who had curled up into a large wing chair.

"Well, Emmie, did you enjoy you first London ball?" he asked, with amused tolerance.

"Very much, sir, but I vow that Almack's is much overrated," she protested. "Did you taste that stale bread and weak lemonade?"

He grinned knowingly. "I wouldn't think of touching that bread and lemonade. That's all a part of the great illusion, you see. Being admitted to Almack's is a privilege, and they don't need to serve decent food to make everyone flock to that Marriage Mart. Starting tomorrow morning, the invitations will pour in, and Grandmama will go through them with you to see which to accept and which to decline. She'll accompany you to a number of the entertainments, but you must watch that she does not tire herself."

Emmeline stifled a yawn. The brandy was making her very relaxed and sleepy.

Charles reached for her empty glass, and gave her a hand out of the chair. "Is Marianne waiting up for you?" he asked.

"I suppose so. I didn't tell her not to." She smiled invitingly. "Did you want to play abigail?" she asked mischievously.

"Minx!" he breathed into her ear. "I'll give you ten minutes and then I'll send her packing."

True to his word, in exactly ten minutes he entered her bedchamber wearing his wine brocade dressing gown, held the door for Marianne to leave, then pulled Emmeline into his arms and waltzed her around the room, holding her much closer than would have been proper earlier in the evening.

"Did anyone tell you that you dance divinely, my love?" he asked, murmuring the words softly into her ear. His breath against that organ caused little sensations of delight and made her unconsciously press closer to the muscles so evident under his thin garment.

The pace of the waltz decreased until it stopped completely and they were in each other's arms, his lips making delicate forays between her mouth and her ear lobe as her fingers struggled to unfasten the sash of his robe. In a stillness that was almost tangible, her arms slid around his neck and his kiss deepened as his tongue gently seduced her and she tasted once more the flavor of old brandy, warm and exciting.

They stood in front of the hearth, their clothing abandoned around their feet. His deep kisses, the feel of his hands as they caressed her bare flesh, and the heat which emanated from the blazing logs combined to make her crazy with need.

She heard herself begging, "Please, Charles . . ." then felt his strength as he swept her up into his arms and placed her tenderly on the bed.

As his roving hands tortured her still more before bringing her joyous relief, she thought fleetingly of her mother and felt sorry for her and the many others like her.

CHARLES'S PROPHECY HAD been correct, and the days that followed became hectic with as many as three and four functions to be attended in one evening. On return to Berkeley Square in the small hours of the morning, Emmeline often almost fell asleep before she reached her bed. Early morning rides in the Park had to be abandoned in order for her to get sufficient rest.

Even when Charles deserted her, his friends and Ariadne made up for his absence, and she sometimes came home to see a light in the library, or Charles standing at the door of that room wishing her a good night.

One bright afternoon she returned from riding in the Park with Lord Peter Fogarty to find that Lady Poole had arrived unexpectedly and was sipping tea with Lady Millford in the drawing room.

"You're looking tired, missy," Lady Poole reproached, after the usual pleasantries had been exchanged. "Your grandmama tells me she sees you no more than an hour or so each day before you're off racketing to dinners, balls, and such every night of the week. I wonder why it is she sees more of her grandson than she does of you, eh?"

Emmeline had forgotten how blunt and outspoken

Lady Poole could be, and was embarrassed that she had asked such a question in front of Lady Millford.

"Lord Charles does not care for many of the entertainments, but he always knows where I am and with whom, my lady." She turned to Lady Millford. "Why, ma'am, you yourself accompanied me to two soirees only last week, and there is to be another tomorrow evening which I believe you are attending."

Lady Millford regarded her granddaughter with a somewhat amused expression on her face. "Her ladyship is only trying to make you feel guilty for not having written to her for so long, as like as not, Emmeline. And I'm glad you reminded me. I'll secure another invitation for tomorrow night and my old friend can accompany us."

"How is Cousin Harriet getting along on her bad ankle, Lady Poole?" Emmeline asked politely.

"Very slowly, my dear. In fact, as I've just been telling Lady Millford, I'm sending her up to Scotland to visit another mutual relative we have there. It'll put a stop to some of the tales she's been telling around about your stay with us." The old lady paused to see the effect of her words as Emmeline looked quite startled.

"She doesn't know the whole story, so she's made it up as she's gone along, and the general idea seems to be that you ran away from home with Lord Charles, then quarreled with him and tried to leave for London. But he found you at Poole House and married you quickly to stop the gossip."

"Did you tell her the true story?" Emmeline asked, quiet now.

"Of course not," snapped Lady Poole. "It's none of her concern and besides, I promised Charles I'd talk to no one about it."

Seeing Emmeline's dismay, Lady Millford reached over and patted her hand. "Now don't start moping,

Emmeline. We'll discuss it with Charles and he'll know exactly how to handle anyone who tries to turn it into something scandalous. When you're seen around with Lady Poole and me, you'll be surprised how quickly any gossip will die." She frowned suddenly. "But you and Charles had better be seen together more. I hadn't realized he'd given you such a long lead. I'll talk to him tonight."

Emmeline's step was lighter as she ascended the stairs. She'd much rather be with Charles than anyone else, and it was possible that Cousin Harriet had unintentionally done her a favor. She just hoped that he wouldn't blame her too much for having enjoyed herself without him.

Fourteen

Emmeline shifted restlessly on one of the small gold chairs carefully placed in rows in Lady Oglethorpe's ballroom as she waited for the introduction to society of an Austrian violinist. His wife, a soprano, accompanied him and also performed. At Emmeline's side was her escort for tonight, Sir John Barrington, who, unknown to her, was one of the two friends of Charles who had helped him in his search for her some months ago.

She had been feeling increasingly tired of late, although she was reluctant to admit it, and tonight the selection of sacred compositions by Bach was too heavy and pious for her to enjoy. She determined to persuade Sir John to leave at the first opportunity and take her to Almack's for an hour or so, but in the meantime politeness demanded that she remain seated and appear attentive.

Quite naturally, her mind wandered to her most important cause for concern, which was not so much Harriet Jones's malicous remarks as Charles's talk with his grandmama. He had looked sternly at her several evenings ago when she had returned home very late, but had made no comment, and she was afraid that Lady Millford's remarks might add fuel to the fire—always assuming a fire was there.

She glanced around the room, observing several of

her friends who seemed as restless as she, then caught sight of a familiar figure standing in the doorway. He saw her looking and nodded in unsmiling greeting. What on earth could Charles be doing at a musicale? He had informed her some time ago that this was precisely the kind of entertainment that bored him to distraction. With a sinking feeling, she turned her attention back to the performers, now hoping that they would continue to play for some time yet, possibly long enough for Charles to become tired of waiting and leave for other interests.

Still deep in thought, she did not realize when the music stopped and the audience applauded politely. It took Sir John's deep voice to bring her back to her surroundings. "Look who's here, Emmeline. I've never seen Charles at an affair of this sort before."

He was coming over to them and they rose and met him halfway. "We were just going to try a little supper, Charles. Would you like to look for a table and I'll bring something back for all of us?" Sir John said as he put an arm around his friend's shoulder and steered them over to a quieter area at the back of the supper room where the more secluded tables were placed.

Once they were seated and Sir John had left to get some food, Emmeline looked up at her husband's still unsmiling face. "Am I to get a scold, Charles?" she asked him, a slight frown creasing her brow.

He still looked serious but his mouth softened a little. "Do you deserve one, my dear?" he asked, looking her over speculatively.

She moistened her lips, irritated at her own nervousness. "I don't think so. I haven't done anything you said I shouldn't," she said, trying to sound more confident than she felt.

"Then you've nothing to look so worried about, have

you?" he said with a flicker of a smile. "Ah, John's been successful."

He rose to help Sir John with the tray of refreshments he carried, then the two of them entered into a lively discussion about some horses Sir John had seen at Tattersall's. They drew her into the conversation, and Charles told Sir John about Thunder and Lovely Lady, bringing some animation back to Emmeline's face, but this disappeared quickly at his next remark.

"If you don't mind, John, I'm going to take Emmeline home before the caterwauling starts once more. It was good of you to escort her to this affair—though why she wanted to come I have no idea—but she's been looking a little peaked lately, and I think she should have an early night."

Emmeline wanted to protest, but a stern glance from Charles took away her courage. Sir John was, of course, all graciousness and apologized for contributing to her fatigue. Taking Emmeline's arm firmly, Charles escorted her to the door and made charming apologies to their hostess for leaving so early.

Though the drive from the Oglethorpe mansion in Grosvenor Square to Berkeley Square was short, it was uncomfortable for Emmeline as she sat in the corner of the carriage and waited for an explanation from Charles that was not forthcoming.

In silence still, he handed her out of the carriage and helped her up the steps to the front door. Once in the hall he released her arm and she started toward the stairs, but his quiet voice stopped her.

"Please join me in the library, my dear. There appears to be a matter we should discuss."

He opened the door to allow her to pass in front of him, then closed it firmly. Taking out a decanter and glasses, he asked, "Brandy?"

She shook her head and took a seat on the edge of a chair facing the desk.

"Relax, Emmie," he said kindly. "You're making me think you've something to feel guilty about, and I'm sure that's not true—yet."

As he spoke he pulled out a footstool, made her sit back in the chair, and propped up her feet. He leaned against the front of the desk and sipped his brandy. Emmeline waited.

"You've already spoken with Lady Poole and Grandmama, so you know what this is all about," he began. "Can you tell me how many times you and I have been out together in the last month?"

"It happened gradually," she said desperately. "You took me places, but then excused yourself and encouraged me to go on to some other place with your friends—"

"That doesn't answer my question, Emmeline," he said.

She shook her head. "I don't know. Not more than three or four, and that right at the beginning."

Charles moved closer and sat on the edge of the footstool.

"Don't look so upset, my love," he murmured. "It's every bit as much my fault as yours. I find it difficult to be interested in the Season for longer than a week. But you missed 'coming out' and I wanted you to enjoy yourself and get it out of your system before you got like my sister and couldn't come to town."

Her eyes widened, and relief started to spread through her. "You mean you're not angry with me?" she asked.

He shrugged. "If I'm angry with you, then I have to also be angry with myself, and there's little point in that. But you've overdone it," he growled softly, "going to as many as three affairs in an evening, and some afternoons as well." The scold was light, but he continued. "You're exhausted and I'm going to insist that you take two days of complete rest—send your regrets where you have commitments. After that, I'll go through all invitations with you and take you to at least one each night. You'll also drive with me in the Park, but I'm sure our friends will join us."

She knew he was right, and she was very tired, but it seemed so much like being sent to her room for two days that she couldn't help the tears that came to her eyes.

"Are you saying I have to stay in my room for the two days, and . . . ?" The tears welled up again and she choked off the sentence.

"Of course not. I'm not punishing you, Emmie," he said softly. "If it'll make you feel better, I'll stay in also and take care of some book work for a couple of days. In the evenings we can play chess."

He stood up and held out his arms, and she went into them gladly, sure now that he held no animosity toward her. It was quite a few minutes before she was able to catch her breath, and then he escorted her, keeping an arm around her waist, up the stairs and into her bedchamber. A moment later, Marianne came out of the room, closing the door quietly behind her, a smile on her usually serious face.

THE TWO DAYS spent at home were as beneficial to Emmeline as Charles had hoped. He instructed Marianne that she was not to be awakened each morning, but left to sleep as long as she could, and breakfast was to be brought to her room after she awoke. After they had luncheon with Lady Millford and Lady Poole, he insisted that she rest for an hour or more and the rings soon disappeared from around her eyes and her skin regained its healthy glow.

Each evening after dinner, Emmeline and Charles

played chess, a game which she had enjoyed from childhood with her father. She proved a worthy opponent, beating Charles the first time, and making him realize her expertise.

On the third day he took her for a drive in the Park in the afternoon, and promised to escort her to a ball in the evening. The friends who accompanied them on their drive sought to book dances with Emmeline, but Charles held firm that he must have all the waltzes.

There had been much teasing between the good friends, and she and Charles were still laughing when they arrived back in Berkeley Square. They noticed a traveling carriage drawn up outside the house, but thought little of it, assuming it to be connected with Lady Poole's visit.

As they entered the house still laughing, Manning, the butler, came toward them.

"You have guests, your lordship. Lady Millford is entertaining a Lady Barrow and her daughter. They have considerable baggage and it appears they have come to stay."

Charles thanked the butler and turned to Emmeline. "Did you invite them to stay here, Emmeline?" he asked, the laughter having frozen into an icy coolness.

But Emmeline's face showed as much surprise as that of Charles.

"No, Charles, never. I wrote them that we were staying here, but I am not in a position to invite anyone to stay in this house. I am a guest myself," she told him, keeping her voice low so as not be heard in the drawing room.

"You're not exactly that, Emmie, but I would expect you to ask before inviting overnight guests." His voice had warmed as soon as he realized this was not of her doing. "We'd better make our presence known and relieve Grandmama."

As they entered the room, Lady Barrow beamed and called, "Emmeline, darling, come and give your mother a big hug. It's been so long since we saw you, my love," and she held out her arms as though hugging her daughter had been a normality when Emmeline lived at home.

Emmeline curtsied to Lady Millford, crossed the room, and submitted briefly to her mother's show of affection, then greeted her sister Agatha, who responded coolly.

Lady Barrow laughed and pointed a finger at Emmeline. "It was very naughty of you to invite us and not let Lady Millford know, darling. It could have been most embarrassing if there'd been a lot of other guests in this huge, beautiful mansion."

Emmeline flushed to the roots of her hair, and turned an appealing glance to Charles for help.

He looked at her searchingly, then turned to Lady Barrow. "There was obviously some misunderstanding," he said smoothly. "How long were you planning to stay in town?"

Lady Barrow flushed at the direct question, but recovered immediately. "Well we really didn't think about it, with the Season and everything. When Emmeline said how lonely she was, we just had to come and make her feel better. Lord Barrow couldn't come with us, but may be in town later."

"Had you given us some notice, we might have been able to change plans, but I fear we will have to leave you to your own devices for the evening as Emmeline and I have a dinner party and ball to attend," he drawled coolly. "Are you and Lady Poole engaged tonight, Grandmama?"

"I'm afraid we are, Charles," she said, sounding regretful, "but I'm sure I can find a free evening to spend with Lady Barrow before she leaves."

"Mrs. Manning will show you to your rooms in the

west wing, Lady Barrow," Charles advised. "I want Emmeline to rest before she has to dress for our engagement, so we'll leave you now and see you in the morning."

He bowed, took Emmeline's arm, and drew her smoothly into the hall and up the staircase to her bedchamber. Not until they were safely in the room with the door closed did he make so much as a murmur, but as soon as they had privacy he swung her around to face him and his hand under her chin forced her to look at him directly.

"I believed you when you said you hadn't invited them, Emmeline, but I don't recall your refuting her remarks about the invitation and your loneliness—though how you could possibly have been lonely with the pace you were setting is beyond my comprehension." He looked very stern and his grip on her chin was hard.

"Please, Charles, you're hurting me." Her words were barely audible, but he released his hold on her immediately. "How could you expect me to tell my own mother that she was lying? I had no wish for them to come here. In fact, it's going to spoil everything, I know."

Her last words were almost a sob.

"No, it's not, for I will not allow it," he said firmly. "They may stay for a week—no more. And in that time they must find a suitable accommodation for themselves. They should have the money. Lord Grantley told my father he had formed a trust to cover dowries and a come-out for all three of his daughters. If your stepfather has broken that trust, then he might be subject to prosecution by law."

He reached for the bell and rang for the abigail, who entered the room almost immediately.

"Marianne, I want Lady Emmeline to rest until it's time to bathe and dress. If either her mother or sister should come to the door, you are to tell them she is sleeping and will see them in the morning. Under no circumstances are you to let them in. Is that clear?" he demanded.

"Perfectly clear, milord," Marianne replied with a faint smile. "I'll see that she gets her rest."

Both Agatha and Lady Barrow tried to see Emmeline but were turned away, and the latter made it perfectly clear that it would not be the last Emmeline heard about it. But they did not try again and Emmeline was able to bathe and dress for the evening without any further disturbance.

They did not stay late at the ball, and on the drive home Emmeline could not but enjoy being held in her husband's strong arms while she rested her head on his shoulder. She was so comfortable, in fact, that he had to waken her when they reached the house.

Charles came to her bedchamber that night, as he had for the last two nights, and she marveled once again at the tenderness such a big man could show her before he overcame every vestige of self-control she possessed. He could make her shamelessly beg for relief, and to her delight had started teaching her how to give him even more pleasure.

When she awoke the next morning, he was already gone, and she lay quietly for some time before ringing for Marianne, trying to decide what she could do about her mother and sister.

It was wasted effort, however, as she was hardly through sipping her hot chocolate when there was a sharp knock on the door and before Marianne could answer it, Lady Barrow entered, dressed in a wrapper and still wearing her nightcap.

Emmeline recovered from her surprise at the intrusion more quickly than her abigail did. "Mother, unless the house is on fire, don't ever enter this room without permission again," she said firmly. "Charles would have been most embarrassed had he still been with me."

Lady Barrow was momentarily taken aback. It had obviously never occurred to her that her son-in-law spent the night with his wife, and she paused long enough for Emmeline to signal Marianne to bring her a dressing gown. She preferred not to be trapped in her bed and forced to listen to her mother's complaints.

Her ladyship intercepted the signal, however, and snatched the wrapper out of Marianne's hands. "I'll take care of that, my girl," she snapped, "and you may leave us for now."

"Just a moment, Mother." Emmeline held up her hands to prevent her mother from assisting her. "As you are here, please take a seat while Marianne helps me dress. His lordship expects me at breakfast very shortly and I should not like to keep him waiting."

Marianne held a chair for Lady Barrow and, defeated once more, there was nothing she could do but sit down gracefully and watch her daughter slip into the wrapper and move over to the dressing table where Marianne waited, towel in hand.

"You know, Emmeline, your sister has not had the advantages that you have, and it is essential she make her come-out this Season or she'll be too old," her ladyship began again, leaning forward in an effort to see her daughter's face. "You have an obligation to help her find a suitable husband—"

Emmeline interrupted. "You know I did not invite you, Mama. And you should realize that Charles will not permit you to stay with us for more than about a week, until you find a place of your own."

Lady Barrow looked meaningly at Marianne, but Emmeline ignored her.

"But that is impossible. Lord Barrow cannot release

the kind of funds we would need to set up on our own," her ladyship protested.

"You have no alternative, Mama," Emmeline said firmly. "Had you written me asking to be invited, I would have talked to Lord Charles and he just might have tried to help. But now he is angry that you should arrive here saying I invited you when he knows it's not true."

"You ungrateful wretch! You mean you denied inviting your own mother here? I'll have a word with him and make sure he believes you asked us. Just you see." She looked as though she would have liked to slap Emmeline had she been closer.

Throughout the conversation Marianne had continued to get Emmeline ready, patting her face dry, arranging her hair, selecting a gown for her to wear, and now she stood back waiting.

"I'm afraid I must ask you to leave me now, Mama, while I finish dressing. I'm sure there will be other opportunities for us to converse," Emmeline said, ignoring her mother's outburst. As she turned to take from Marianne a note that had just been hand-delivered, she missed the speculative expression on her mother's face. She glanced at Ariadne's note, then dropped it onto a table.

Her ladyship became petulant. "The very least you can do, Emmeline, is introduce us to your dressmaker. Agatha must have gowns made quickly, and only an introduction by a customer would ensure such promptness," she said with a sigh.

Emmeline shrugged. That was little enough, and surely Charles would not object. "Of course, Mama. As a matter of fact my friend, Lady Ariadne Graham, has just confirmed our plans to visit Madame Rolande this very morning. Perhaps you and Agatha would care to accompany us?"

Lady Barrow dropped her handkerchief and bent to pick it up. She had gained her objective so she rose quickly saying, "We would be delighted. I must go and tell Agatha to get ready right away," and hurried from the room, but not before slipping the kerchief with Lady Ariadne's note concealed in it into the pocket of her wrapper.

THE FOUR LADIES stepped out of the Graham carriage at Madame Rolande's and Emmeline made the introductions. Her own business with the dressmaker was conducted quickly and, as it seemed that Lady Barrow and Agatha would be some time, Emmeline and Lady Ariadne took the carriage to complete their other shopping, promising to return for the others in an hour.

During the drive Lady Barrow, backed strongly by Agatha, had been most outspoken and critical of her younger daughter, completely without cause, and Emmeline had retained a quiet dignity throughout. Now, however, she found herself so nervous that it was very nearly impossible to make a decision about the smallest selection, and finally she decided to make her purchases on another day.

Her friend, although noticing her distress, had said nothing to this point, but now couldn't help but comment. "It's very strange, Emmeline, you're not the slightest bit like your mother or your sister in appearance or anything else. Don't let them hurt you and upset you," she advised. "Your sister seems to bear you a grudge. Above all, don't let them come between you and Charles."

"They won't be here for long, Ariadne." Emmeline smiled with relief at her friend's words. "Charles says they must leave in a week. They were not invited, you know."

"Well, that's good news. They're going to rent a house of their own?" Ariadne asked.

"I suppose they are," Emmeline said hesitantly, then added, "But of course they must intend to. Why else would they be buying so many clothes for Agatha?"

When the four returned to the house they found Charles was at his club, so they joined the two dowagers for a light luncheon.

EMMELINE HAD TO admit that Charles was being very patient with his in-laws. Having agreed that they could stay for a week, he seemed determined to be as pleasant as possible, and even allowed them to accompany her, himself, and the two dowagers to a couple of affairs large enough for him to secure them invitations at such short notice.

She saw his look of surprise at the fashionable dresses they both wore on these occasions, and felt pleased that the introduction to Madame Rolande had been such a success. But she was quite sure they had made no effort all week to find a suitable house to rent. A coach had been put at their disposal on more than one occasion, but they had returned each time laden with parcels and no mention was made of anything except their shopping.

On the evening of their fifth day with them, it seemed Charles could wait no longer, and he questioned her about this.

"I really don't know if they've done anything at all about a house, Charles, but I hardly think so. Would you like me to question Mother?" she asked, trying to be helpful.

He shook his head. "If they have said nothing to you about a house, then they have not looked for one. I don't want you to become involved, so I'll talk to your mother myself tomorrow," he said sharply. "There's another matter I wish to talk to her about, the matter of the trust your father left for his daughters."

"You didn't get anything at all from Lord Barrow?"

"No, he made some vague murmurings about your father's man of business having passed on and he'd have to speak with his successor. I've been intending to have a strongly worded letter sent to him. This should save me the time," he said grimly.

True to his word, on the following day Emmeline heard him request a few words with Lady Barrow in the library, but the walls were thick and no sounds would have been heard even if they were murdering each other.

She and Agatha, having exhausted polite conversation, were looking through copies of *The Ladies' Monthly Museum* when Lady Barrow burst into the room, her face flushed and tearstained.

"I have never been so insulted in all my life!" she half-cried, half-screamed. "Come, Agatha, we're leaving this house just as soon as we have our luggage together." She turned to Emmeline, who with Agatha had crossed toward her mother. "And as for you, you deserve all you'll get from that husband of yours when he turns on you, you ungrateful, insolent baggage."

Emmeline was struck hard across the face before she realized what her mother was about to do, and she staggered back from the unexpected blow.

When she could no longer hear them on the stairs, she went slowly up to her bedchamber. One look in the mirror told her that she'd have to stay home tonight. Her cheek was already showing an ugly bruise.

A request for a luncheon tray upstairs brought Charles also, curious to find out what was wrong, and when he saw her face he was furious.

"Did my family already leave, Charles?" Emmeline asked, trying to ignore her throbbing cheek.

"Yes they did, and if I'd seen you before her ladyship left, she'd have had more than my harsh words to go with," he snarled.

"Oh, you surely don't think . . ." she started, trying to pretend that it was an accident.

He grabbed her shoulders roughly, and shook her. "Don't you ever lie to me again!" he thundered. "She showed me the note you sent, with the Millford crest, inviting them to spend the Season with us. I know from which side of your family you got that habit."

He released his grasp so suddenly that she had to reach for the bedpost as she lost her balance, and as he stormed out of the room she slid slowly to the floor, holding her aching head in her hands. She remembered then how clever Agatha had always been at copying other people's writing, and knew who had written that note.

Fifteen

One of the things Emmeline had been missing in the magnificent townhouse was a place where she could be completely alone. There were innumerable such places in the country, where the estate surrounded the house and it was relatively easy to escape for a few hours and still be perfectly safe. But here in London, it was not safe for a lady to venture outdoors unless accompanied on foot by a maid, on horseback by a groom, and in a carriage by another female, a suitable gentleman, or a maid, and of course, one or more footmen.

In the house it seemed that there were always maids and footmen underfoot performing their myriad duties, and when they were absent the butler or the housekeeper came to check that their work had been done properly. Even in her own bedchamber when Marianne was not busy there, maids would come to poke fires, turn down beds, or clean.

It thus became necessary for Emmeline to find a secret place where she could be alone with her thoughts and where no one would disturb her. To this end, she proceeded to search the house from top to bottom, and finally found what she was looking for. On the third floor, adjacent to one of the bedrooms not in regular use, she found a small room with a large window, possibly intended for a young child's use, and there was a key in the door which she could turn and leave in the lock so that no one could enter.

She could not ask the housekeeper to have the room cleaned without revealing her secret hideaway, so she spent several hours in the next few days cleaning and polishing it herself until the floors and furniture shone. Then she dragged a comfortable chair inside and borrowed a few books from the library.

While Lady Millford was resting and Charles was out with his cronies, she would steal away to her secret place and sit there peacefully reading or just watching the traffic going around the square. The trees in the square would soon be bare, but the branches were graceful and she could imagine how lovely they would be when covered with the first snow. Sometimes young children accompanied by their nannies would play tag or blindman's buff on the smooth grass beyond the trees, and she would delight in watching them laughing and enjoying themselves in a way only the very young can.

After her mother and sister had stormed out of the house, and Lady Poole had gone home to Warwickshire, things returned to normal on the surface, but underneath a cold undercurrent existed between Emmeline and Charles that had not been there before. He continued to take her riding in the Park most afternoons, when they also saw a number of friends, and during her discussion of the various invitations with him he agreed to take her to many of the festivities. But more and more frequently he would be out of town when the time came and she got back into the habit of joining Lady Ariadne and allowing one of Charles's friends to bring her home.

Since the day her mother left, Charles had avoided her bedchamber, and in self-defense Emmeline started to flirt a little with the men who paid her compliments, and posies were sometimes sent to her which did not come from one of Charles's friends. The cool distance between her and Charles seemed to grow daily, and in her unhappiness she sought the seclusion of her secret place more frequently.

She had not been feeling well, and she had missed her monthly course twice now, but as she was losing rather than gaining weight she decided her own unhappiness and lack of appetite must be the cause.

At luncheon one day when Emmeline and Lady Millford happened to be dining alone, the dowager questioned her. "It seems to me there's something gone very sour between you and my grandson, Emmeline, and it's been that way ever since that mother of yours was here," she remarked, looking at her severely. "I don't hear you arguing, but I don't hear you making up either. Maybe a good quarrel would do you both a world of good and clear the air between you."

Emmeline made no response, but the very next day the dowager had her wish. Ariadne had called and she and Emmeline had gone shopping during the morning. Refusing an invitation to luncheon, Ariadne dropped Emmeline back at the house and a footman came out to carry in the packages.

No sooner had Emmeline entered the hall than the library door swung open and Charles stood in the opening.

"Would you mind joining me for a few moments, my lady?" he asked politely. "There seems to be a small matter we need to discuss."

With a questioning look, she complied with his request, taking the same seat as on a previous occasion, directly across from the desk. She looked at his unsmiling face, trying to read from the compressed lips and half-closed eyes to what extent she had supposedly transgressed this time.

"I was under the impression—correct me if I'm wrong," he started in a coldly sarcastic tone, "that most of your gowns were purchased when we first arrived in town. There have been perhaps one or two since, but no more than that, to my knowledge."

Emmeline gave him an icy stare. "I don't understand what you mean, my lord. You yourself placed the order for most of my gowns, as you say, when we first arrived in town. In addition, I had a costume made more than a month ago for the Overton's masquerade. I cannot believe that its price was enough to cause you such concern."

He flung a number of bills into her lap. "Then tell me what this is all about, if you please," he demanded, harshly.

She looked at the neat handwriting of Madame Rolande and, as she saw the dates and counted more than forty garments, she realized the trick her mother had played on her. She tried to meet his angry eyes, but had to turn away. "I know you won't believe me, sir, but I did not tell the dressmaker to charge these to your account. All I did was introduce my mother and ask that she render her assistance."

"I have already spoken to Madame Rolande and she says that you told her to bill me for these items. Is she lying or are you?" His voice was so cold it made her shiver.

"How can you believe I would let them charge their clothes to you?" Emmeline protested. "You can ask Ariadne. She was there when I made the introduction that day."

"I would not think of bringing someone outside the family into a matter of this sort," he said scornfully. "I have told Madame Rolande that I am not responsible for these bills and have advised her to send them to Lord Barrow."

Emmeline knew there was something that in her present confusion she was completely missing. Then she realized what it was.

"But, my lord, how could they possibly have obtained so many garments in the one week they were here?" She looked again at the dates on the bills. "These gowns were made just these last two weeks. I don't understand."

"Don't you? You mean you don't visit them when you disappear for hours at a time without telling anyone where you are going? And without taking a maid?" He went on, his calm becoming even deadlier. "If you don't visit your mother and sister, who do you meet with, Emmeline?"

She sighed heavily. "I can see it's no use my trying to tell you anything. You're not going to believe me, no matter what I say."

She looked into his stern face, in her own distress not seeing the lines of pain there. If he was so suspicious of her movements, she would have to stop stealing away to her secret refuge, and without it London would be impossible.

"Please take me home, Charles," she begged, with almost a sob in her voice. "Perhaps we could be happy again if we went back to Warwickshire."

"You did not answer my question. Who are you slipping out to see?" he demanded.

"I have already told you," she said wearily, "I am not seeing anyone. Now do you mind if I go and change for luncheon?"

Without another word, he opened the door for her to leave.

To Emmeline's surprise, Charles's manner following his accusations changed very little from what it had been of late. He continued to drive her in the Park on occasion, and to take her to several social functions, as before.

She could not help but wonder where in London her mother and sister were staying, and thought it strange that she had not seen them about town. She felt it probable, however, that by now Lord Barrow had joined them, and since he had a great many friends in London, some of whom had visited him in Yorkshire quite frequently, they were probably staying with one of them.

One morning as she was breakfasting alone, Manning brought a note from Lady Ariadne. "The boy would not wait for a reply, my lady," he told her.

She quite frequently received notes from her friend, but it was most unusual for the messenger not to wait for her response. Curious, she opened the missive and read the hastily scrawled words asking her urgently to meet Ariadne at three o'clock that afternoon. She specified a place quite close to one of the entrances to the Park.

Had Charles returned before she needed to leave, she would have shown him the letter, but he did not come back to the house for luncheon and at half past two she made the decision to keep the appointment. It was not very far away, and she felt like some exercise, so she set out on foot, accompanied by her abigail, but as she approached the meeting place she told Marianne to stay just out of sight, for the tone of the note suggested something very confidential.

When she had waited five minutes and Ariadne had not arrived, she became worried and was about to return home when a man on horseback approached. His face seemed vaguely familiar, but she could not remember where she'd seen him before. His manner, however, was almost audacious as he dismounted, tied his horse to a fence, and came toward her.

Alarmed, she turned to call Marianne, but he caught her arm and swung her around.

"Not so fast, Lady Emmeline," he said with an oily smile. "I have a message from Lady Ariadne."

He stood there, holding her arm and smiling, as though waiting for something. Several riders and carriages passed them and entered the Park, but in her anxiety Emmeline scarcely noticed them. She felt sure there must be something very wrong if Ariadne sent this man.

"Has something happened to Lady Ariadne?" she asked anxiously.

"Not to the best of my knowledge," he said with a shrug of his shoulders. "She asked me to let you know she couldn't meet you and said she'll contact you again. That's all, and I must say, it's been a pleasure, your ladyship." He released her arm and bowed mockingly before returning to his mount.

Suddenly aware of the compromising position in which she had placed herself, Emmeline hastened back to where Marianne was patiently waiting and they returned to the house without further incident.

She was still worrying about her friend when Sir John Barrington arrived to escort her to yet another party. She was relieved to see Lady Ariadne in attendance, but it was not until almost the end of the evening that she managed to get her friend alone for a moment. All evening, Lady Ariadne had been looking at her very strangely, as though Emmeline had been the one to break the appointment, and Emmeline couldn't contain her curiosity as to the reason.

"Is something wrong, Ariadne?" she asked. "You've been looking at me all evening as though I and not you was the one who didn't keep our appointment today."

In her concern regarding Emmeline's reputation, Ariadne completely missed the reference to a meeting.

"It's just that I can't imagine you with Miles Frobisher," she burst out. "What Charles will say when he hears, I hate to think. And he will hear, my dear. It won't be one of us, but someone will tell him they saw you." She gave her an embarrassed little smile.

Before Emmeline could ask what she meant, her partner for the next dance was there, and she had no further opportunity to see her friend again alone.

Sir John was very quiet on the drive home, and she finally asked him the question she had meant to ask Ariadne. "Do you know who Miles Frobisher is, John?"

"Not intimately," he told her, "but it looked very much as though you did today."

"Was that the man who grabbed hold of my arm near the entrance to the Park?" she asked him.

"You didn't appear to be exactly struggling to get away, Emmeline," he returned wryly.

She sighed. "It seems that everything I do lately goes wrong. Let me tell you what happened, for I fear that when Charles hears about the meeting, he won't even listen to my side."

After she told him about Ariadne's note, and the conversation between her and the man on horseback, he shook his head sadly. "It looks very much as though someone set a trap for you, my dear. Are you sure it was Ariadne's writing? Just to be seen alone talking to someone of Frobisher's ilk could ruin you socially. Do you know anyone with a reason to hold a grudge?" he asked finally.

"Only my stepfather, my mother, and my sister. They charged all their clothes for the Season to Charles's account. He refused to pay it and sent the bill to Lord Barrow. I didn't know they had stayed in town, and still do not have their direction." She gave a pathetic little laugh. "You'd better drive once more around the square. I doubt that Charles will allow me out again when he hears about my meeting with such a rake. Does the man really have such a bad reputation, John?"

"The worst possible," he confirmed dismally. "No decent girl would be found within a mile of him."

They had reached the house now, and he offered to come inside with her in case Charles was home, but she declined, accepting a hand out of the carriage, then walking slowly up the steps to the front door.

As Manning took her cloak, she asked if his lordship was in the library, and when he confirmed this, she decided to beard the lion in his den. Charles was sitting at his desk, a glass of brandy in his hand, looking sadly into the fire as she opened the door quietly and stepped inside. His expression changed to cold indifference when he saw her.

"I don't remember asking you to come in," he said icily. "I've not decided what to do about you yet, so I think we'd better leave it until morning."

Even though his attitude was expected, she had to blink back tears. "That's just what I told John a few minutes ago," she said, slowly shaking her head. "You're not even interested in my explanation."

"Just answer me one question," he demanded. "Is Frobisher the one you've been sneaking out to see?"

"I told you before," she said, angry now, "I've not been sneaking out to meet anyone. What kind of a fool do you think I am if I would deliberately meet someone of his sort in a place where everyone could see me?"

She knew it was useless to expect an answer so she turned on her heel and slowly left the room, resisting the temptation to slam the door. Ariadne had not denied making the appointment with her. Perhaps she'd hear from her in the morning with some perfectly logical explanation.

* * *

THE NEXT DAY she waited for word from Ariadne, but no message arrived.

Charles had breakfasted early and then left the house, leaving word that he would not be returning for lunch. He had given her no instructions to remain indoors, so she decided to make a trip to the lending library, and ordered the carriage for herself and Marianne for two-thirty. She did not expect to be very long, just enough time to exchange her books, and it seemed best under the circumstances, that the abigail remain in the carriage directly outside the library door. It was early, and she took her time in exchanging the books she had brought for new ones.

When she was finished, to her amazement she saw her sister coming into the room. Agatha waved and came toward her, looking very smart in a dove-gray redingote and bonnet, and appearing much more friendly than she'd been in a couple of years. With both her husband and her best friend behaving coolly toward her, Emmeline reacted less suspiciously toward her sister's friendly overtures than she would otherwise have done. She greeted Agatha with a faint smile, then asked after her mother.

"She's been ill, but is feeling a little better today. She's very anxious to see you, Emmeline, to explain how the dressmaker made a mistake in charging our clothes to Lord Charles," Agatha said, looking rather sheepish. "If you've finished, why don't you come back with me and cheer her up a little. We're not staying very far from here."

"Very well. The Millford carriage is waiting outside and can take us to wherever you're staying." Emmeline replied. She still felt wary of her sister's friendliness, but knew she'd be safe with Marianne accompanying her in the Millford equipage.

A smiling Agatha took her arm, and they stepped out

into the street, but there was no sign of the Millford carriage. Emmeline couldn't understand what had happened, as she was sure she had made her instructions quite clear that they were to wait.

They stood looking up and down the street for some minutes, then Agatha waved to someone and pulled Emmeline toward the road. "Don't bother about your carriage," she said. "We can get a lift from my friend, and afterward the coachman can bring you back here to find out what happened. It's not very far away."

Although assuming that Agatha's friend was a lady, Emmeline still went hesitantly toward the closed coach that had pulled into the curb. She was about to step inside when she realized the sole occupant was her *bête noire* of the previous day, Miles Frobisher.

Agatha gave her a none too gentle push. "Go along, get inside, Emmeline, you've met Mr. Frobisher a number of times, you goose, and he won't bite you."

Had her sister not been so close behind her, Emmeline would never have entered the coach. It was too much of a coincidence to meet this man two days in a row. Suddenly she remembered where she'd seen him before—he was a friend of her stepfather and had stayed at the Range several times. She recalled that Agatha had seemed to be quite smitten by him. Suddenly she was very frightened, but there was nothing she could do now but go along with them and wait.

It seemed that Mr. Frobisher had little to say on this occasion as he sat across from them, smiling at both ladies and making monosyllabic responses to Agatha's prattle. Emmeline had forgotten how foolish conversations had always been between her older sister and members of the opposite sex, but she felt it necessary to try to concentrate on Agatha's remarks, and did not realize how long she had been in the coach until it stopped in a quiet neighborhood of smaller row houses.

She knew her mother would never reside in such an unfashionable area, but she made no comment as Agatha and Mr. Frobisher got out and almost hustled her into one of the houses and up a flight of stairs.

The room they entered was shabby, smelling of stale tobacco and badly in need of a good cleaning. Agatha indicated a chair by the side of the fireplace and, though it was the cleanest of any in the room, Emmeline sat down gingerly. When Frobisher also took a seat, it seemed her fears were confirmed.

"I'll go and see if mother is awake yet, and have the maid bring in some tea." Agatha was almost out of the room as she spoke, and within a few minutes a slatternly young woman came in with a tea tray.

Emmeline's parched throat made the tray look more appetizing than she would have believed, and she was glad when her sister returned to say that her mother was getting up and would come down for tea, but they were not to wait for her. Now she would find out why she was here.

Agatha poured and handed a cup to her and Emmeline sipped the hot beverage gratefully, even though it seemed much more bitter tea than the oolong to which she was accustomed. Then Agatha rose, saying she'd just go and see what was keeping their mother. It had never occurred to Emmeline that her own sister would drug her—at least not until Agatha's voice sounded far away, and she found it a struggle to keep her eyelids open.

But instead of her mother coming through the door, it was her stepfather, only there seemed to be three of him, and then the room started going around. She felt a sharp pain in her leg as the remains of the hot tea spilled onto her lap, then she knew nothing more.

* * *

Sir John Barrington was a better friend of both Emmeline and her husband than either realized. He had close connections with Bow Street and the London police, and it was he who had hired detectives to try to find her when Emmeline had run away. She might not have been able to convince Charles that she was telling the truth about her encounter with Miles Frobisher, but she had convinced Sir John when he had escorted her home the previous evening.

There had been something that didn't ring true about the whole incident, and having done some unsuccessful amateur detective work for the authorities from time to time, he decided that the supposedly innocent meeting could bear some investigation. The place to start was with Emmeline, for if something was afoot, she was sure to be approached a second time.

He decided to ask her a few more questions about her meeting yesterday, and in the early afternoon he stopped by the Millford residence. Manning informed him that he had just missed Lady Emmeline as she had left in the carriage for the lending library. Manning was quite familiar with his lordship's friends, and Sir John had always been a favorite, so he had no qualms about telling him where her ladyship had gone.

"Her ladyship told me that she received a note yesterday, and I was wondering if you might remember what the messenger looked like, Manning. I know you have an excellent memory for faces, and I'm curious," Sir John explained.

"It was just a young errand boy, maybe twelve or thirteen years old," he said. "Kind of sharp, thin nose, and red hair under a very dirty cap. He had on a worn-out jacket, with both elbows through, and I noticed because I couldn't understand why the likes of him was delivering a note from Lady Ariadne."

Sir John glanced sharply at Manning. "Doesn't she usually send a footman?" he asked.

"Yes, sir, and he always waits for an answer," the butler informed him.

With hurried thanks, Sir John got back into his curricle. His tiger released his hold on the horses and jumped nimbly on the back, and Sir John drove off in the direction of the lending library.

He passed the Millford carriage waiting outside for Emmeline, and pulled over some distance away so that he could watch to see what, if anything, happened.

He did not have to wait more than a minute when he saw Miles Frobisher talking to a dark-haired young lady dressed in gray. They seemed to be on intimate terms, Frobisher giving the girl a warm hug while she gazed at him almost worshipfully.

They both entered the lending library, but it could only have been a few seconds later that Frobisher came back out and strolled over to the coachman of the Millford carriage. He spoke to him for a few minutes as if conveying a message, and the man shrugged, tipped his hat, and drove away.

Frobisher then went over to an unmarked, closed carriage some distance down the street and stepped inside, but the coachman made no attempt to move.

There were a number of people, mostly ladies, going in and out of the lending library, and Sir John had to keep a very close eye on the door. He was cursing himself for not asking what Lady Emmeline was wearing when he saw the young lady in gray come out, her arm through Emmeline's.

Both ladies looked up and down the street, and he saw Emmeline frown and shake her head. There was no doubt from her bewildered expression that she couldn't imagine where her carriage had gone to.

He felt as if he were watching a play as the unmarked

carriage started forward, the lady in gray waved to the man inside, and then the carriage drew up to where they were standing. Emmeline started to step in, saw the occupant and hesitated, then was given a firm push by the other girl.

With suspicions aroused, Sir John let the carriage go past, then proceeded to follow it at a safe distance through the city streets until it entered a quiet, middle-class neighborhood and stopped outside one of the houses. Staying far enough away as not to be observed, he told his tiger to stroll casually along the street and make a note of the house number. After the tiger returned, Sir John scribbled a note for the tiger to take to Charles, telling him to come, armed, to this address right away, and look for Sir John's curricle. If he was not there, he'd somehow leave a message for him.

Sir John did not anticipate a long wait, and once the tiger had left, he looked around for a likely street urchin. As he started to unharness one of the horses, a young boy of about eleven stood watching him curiously. Beckoning to the boy, Sir John took out a gold coin and prepared to write another note to Charles. It was a chance, but one he must take.

The coin was pocketed with dexterity, and the youngster solemnly promised to stay with the curricle until a certain gent arrived. That gent would then give him a second gold coin in exchange for the note Sir John would write momentarily.

Less than a minute later, Frobisher's coach driver came out of the house carrying a seemingly unconscious Emmeline, and put her into the unmarked carriage. An older well-dressed man also entered the carriage. As the vehicle took off down the street, Sir John scribbled another note to Charles, advising him which direction to take. Then he mounted his horse and took off after the carriage, praying that Charles would soon be on his way.

Sixteen

On his return to Berkeley Square, Charles was in no better a frame of mind than when he had left earlier that morning. He was still undecided as to what to do about Emmeline. Her approach to him in the library the previous night had had the effect she desired, if in fact she wished to make him doubt her guilt.

Manning had told him that she had left more than two hours ago for the lending library, but once there had sent word to the coachman and her abigail that she would not need them further this afternoon. She had sent no message, however, as to what time she would return, and this was unusual, for she was normally very considerate of the staff and always let Mrs. Manning know whether she would be in for tea.

He went into the drawing room, where his grandmama was presiding over the tea tray.

"Well, at least you have not deserted me today, Charles," she announced, reaching for a cup and saucer. "I can't understand where Emmeline can be. She always leaves word if she is going to take tea out."

"I don't think Emmeline is quite herself of late, Grandmama," he murmured, seeing no reason to have her ladyship angry with Emmeline also.

"Of course she's not herself, my boy," she agreed. "How could you expect her to be when she's increasing?"

"She's what?" Charles thundered, suddenly angry. "Why is it that I'm the last to know? She's never mentioned a word to me!"

"Don't get yourself all upset, Charles. She's not mentioned it to me either, but I can tell the signs. It's always possible that she doesn't realize it herself yet."

There was a loud hammering on the front door knocker and Manning came in bearing a note for Charles.

"A message from Sir John Barrington, your lordship. His tiger is in the kitchen having a bite of food while you get ready, then he says he can show you some place or other." He shrugged helplessly at the strange message.

It was just a folded piece of paper, obviously written in a hurry, the wording further expressing the need for haste.

Charles reached the door before the butler was out of the hall. "Manning, get word to the stable to saddle Jupiter immediately—no, I need to take the tiger with me. Make it my curricle instead, and tell them to be sharp about it. And tell them to put a saddle in the back in case I need to ride."

He took the stairs in great strides, two at a time, and in less than five minutes he was back, carrying a pair of pistols, a beaver hat, and an overcoat. The tiger was just entering the hall from the servants' quarters when the door knocker sounded again, and an envelope was pushed under the door.

Charles grabbed the envelope and flung open the door, but the sound of running footsteps was the only sign that anyone had been near.

Cursing softly, he closed the door and tore open the envelope. The note was printed in block letters and stated that if he wanted to see his wife alive, he was to get thirty thousand pounds together and be ready to take it where the next note instructed.

He thrust it in his pocket, and turned to the tiger.

"Are you ready? Do you think you can show me where Sir John is?" he asked grimly.

"Yes, milord. That I can . . ." But before the tiger could finish, Charles was pushing him ahead and out of the front door where the curricle was waiting.

THE FIRST FEELING Emmeline had as consciousness started to return was a pounding in her head, matched by the sound of horses' hooves traveling at a fast clip, and jostling as the poorly upholstered carriage swung from side to side.

She kept her eyes closed tightly as her memory came slowly back. She remembered her sister giving her a cup of tea, and her own belated realization that it had been drugged. She was about to open her eyes and see if anyone was with her in the carriage when she remembered seeing her stepfather's face just before she lost consciousness. If he had arranged her kidnapping, for that was all it could be, he must mean to exchange her for a large ransom. A tremor of fear passed through her as she thought of what Lord Barrow might do to her before he let her go.

Suddenly a hand grabbed her shoulder viciously and swung her into a sitting position as a familiar voice snarled, "So you finally came around, did you? I was wondering if that stupid sister of yours had been too generous with the laudanum. Have you any idea where we're going, girl?"

Her head almost exploded as he struck her a hard blow.

"Wake up and answer me when I ask you something. You never did learn how to mind me, but you will tonight before I've finished with you."

There was little light in the carriage, but his voice had the thick sound of too much brandy, and she could smell it when he leaned in her direction.

"No," she said, "I've no idea where you're taking me or why—but I expect it's for money."

"You're damned right it's for money, and lots of it," he snarled. "The only good thing you ever did in your life was get that young lord interested enough to marry you. Now he's going to pay and pay well to get you back. But you'll never be able to show your face again anywhere in London. Thanks to Miles Frobisher, the latest *on-dit* has it that you've gone off with him. Tonight it'll be the talk of Almack's and your name will be dirt after that."

"In that case, why would Charles pay to get me back?" she managed to ask, her headache changing rapidly to nausea.

"Because he'll know you didn't go with Frobisher, but he won't be able to prove it," the venomous voice went on. "I want him to know who's behind it, getting revenge for his damned insults."

"But what does Agatha get out of it all? Won't my ruined reputation tarnish her also?" Emmeline asked, trying to keep him talking as long as possible.

"She gets her lover, Frobisher, and a third of the ransom between them. She never wanted a come-out, that was just your mother's idea. All Agatha ever really wanted was Miles, and now they're having their fun, and waiting until Carruthers hands over the money."

He watched her startled face, and his laugh was evil.

"And once we're out of this rattle-trap carriage and into the house that's been readied in Dover, I'm going to have a little fun myself. That husband of yours is going to get nothing but soiled goods for his money, soiled and very sore by the time I finish that whipping I started."

He took a flask out of his pocket and had another swig from it before settling back in his corner again.

* * *

Sir John was keeping well back from the carriage. It was obviously on the road to Dover, and going at a fast pace, but he had no difficulty keeping it in view. Although it was night by now, a full moon was lighting the way.

He had no worry about the kidnappers hearing him, as the noise of their horses' hooves blotted out all other sound. So much so that a rider coming up behind was almost upon him before he even knew he was there. With relief he saw it was Charles, and they rode together, keeping the coach in view while Sir John brought Charles up to date.

"She may not be conscious, Charles. They had to carry her out to the carriage, I'm afraid," he told his friend, "and then the older man got in with her."

"Then it's not Frobisher we're following?" Charles asked. "I felt sure he must be involved in this."

"He was in the beginning. He sent your carriage away, then came up in one of his own to give them a ride. The girl he was with was very attractive, black hair, very shapely, and a little older than Emmeline, I would say. She and Frobisher behaved as though they were, at the very least, lovers. Emmeline seemed to know the girl very well." Sir John was trying to remember anything that would give a clue as to who the kidnappers were.

"That description fits her sister as well as anyone," Charles said, thinking back to Madame Rolande's bill.

"Well, you know, Emmeline thought she was meeting Lady Ariadne yesterday afternoon, when Frobisher showed up instead," Sir John offered. "And Lady Ariadne swears she sent no note."

"So that was it! Incredible though it may sound, I'll warrant her family's behind this. While my butler and footmen were in the room her father threatened to ruin her. What's the man in the carriage like, John? Could you get a close enough look?"

"Tall and thin, probably in his forties, and his clothes were right up to the mark. He didn't soil his hands carrying her. The coachman had to do that. Does that sound like anyone you know?"

"So much so that we'd better stop that coach and get her out before he gets his hands on her, if he hasn't already. It's her stepfather, John, and he's liable to half-kill her, given the chance." Charles reached in his pocket and handed one of the pistols to his friend. "Take this. It's loaded and don't hesitate to use it. I've a mind to play highwayman if you'll join me. You take the coachman and I'll take the inside."

There was a curve in the road far ahead, and the two horsemen took a short cut across country, arriving at the road again a little ahead of the swaying carriage. They only just had time to knot kerchiefs over their faces to better look the part and then John fired over the horses' heads. The coachman struggled to bring them to a halt as a voice rang out.

"Stand and deliver! Your money or your life!"

AS THE CARRIAGE lurched to a halt, Emmeline saw her stepfather reach into his pocket, and then the door nearest her swung open. A shot rang out and the gun Lord Barrow had drawn fell to the floor from his shattered hand.

"I was hoping you'd do that, Barrow. The idea of handing you over to the law unharmed was intolerable."

As he spoke, Charles pulled her stepfather roughly out of the carriage and flung him on the ground. Sir John had already tied up the coachman with his own belt, and now he took charge of Lord Barrow while Emmeline stepped shakily out of the carriage and into her husband's arms.

"Thank God you found me, Charles," she managed to sob before his lips silenced her in the most satisfactory manner. His hands were stroking her back in the soothing way she knew so well, and finally her trembling ceased.

"Did he hurt you at all, darling?" Charles asked, holding her away from him to take a good look, and when he saw the bruise on her temple, his boot made a satisfactory contact with Lord Barrow's ribs as he lay sprawled on the ground.

Between the aftereffects of the drugs and relief after her ordeal, Emmeline was a little hazy as to how she got back to Berkeley Square and tucked comfortably into bed. She only knew that she traveled securely in Charles's arms the whole way, and it was with reluctance that he handed her into his grandmama's care while he and Sir John made the necessary formal charges before a magistrate at Bow Street.

The dowager had been too worried to go to bed, but she was made of stern stuff and had the staff running around in the small hours of the morning, bringing hot water for bathing her granddaughter and warm bricks for her bed lest she catch a chill from her dreadful experience.

A tearful Marianne, heartsick that she had let her mistress go into the library alone, undressed and gently bathed Emmeline while Lady Millford ordered a special posset prepared to help her granddaughter sleep.

News of the arrest of Lord Barrow and Miles Frobisher successfully quashed the rumors they had maliciously started, and from early the next morning flowers were delivered to the house, along with notes from sympathetic friends.

Just before luncheon Manning took a sobbing chambermaid to see Charles in the library. She had worked for the Barrows during their stay, she confessed, and had been bribed by Agatha to let her know each time Emmeline ordered the coach, where it was going, and what time. The maid was dismissed, and another piece of the puzzle fell into place.

Charles had called in an eminent doctor who confirmed that Emmeline was a little too thin but unharmed by her ordeal, and should produce a healthy son or daughter in a little over six months' time.

Dinner that evening was a delightful meal served just to Charles and Emmeline alone in the sitting room of their suite. It reminded her fondly of the other occasion when they had dined in similar fashion. She was concerned about leaving the dowager to dine alone, but Charles assured her that her ladyship had received at least a dozen last-minute invitations for this evening from curious friends, and in the end had allowed herself to be wined and dined by an old beau.

When the table had been cleared and Charles was drinking his brandy, and Emmeline had curled up comfortably in the crook of his arm, he made a vow that they'd never come to such a pass again. "We were getting along so well, love, before we arrived in London. How on earth did we reach a point where you couldn't talk to me and I wouldn't listen if you did?" He dropped a kiss on her forehead.

"Everything was all right until Mother and Agatha arrived, if you remember," Emmeline remarked. "I recall your saying that we wouldn't let them spoil things for us, but they did."

"Yes, they certainly did. The day I told your mother to leave, she told me that we had a duty to bring out Agatha, and that Lord Barrow had spent all the money left in trust for the three of you, so it was now my obligation." He laughed. "You can imagine how well that went over wth me. I sent her packing fast and even threatened to sue Lord Barrow on your behalf for using money left in trust."

"You do believe me now, don't you, that I never invited Mother and Agatha to visit, nor said they could charge the gowns to you?" Emmeline was anxious to get this and a few other matters aired and cleared up.

"Of course, darling. I think I knew at the time, but I was just so angry I couldn't see clearly. Forgive me, dearest," he asked, his fingers playing havoc with her emotions as they trailed slowly around her ear and down her neck.

"Mm," she murmured, "Agatha wrote that letter and also this one supposedly from Ariadne, I'm sure. She was gifted that way," she told him and he nodded. "And now there's something I have to beg your forgiveness for, and secure your promise to forget it ever happened. You must begin to trust me again." As she spoke she looked up into his eyes searchingly.

"Of course. What is it, love?" he asked gently.

"A long time ago I lied to you. I ran away when I had promised I wouldn't. I have never lied to you since, and I never will again, but it hurts when you use it against me and call me a liar." This was very important to her, and she waited for his response.

"I forgave you long ago for that, but I obviously didn't forget. The slate's clean, love. I know you don't lie and I give you my word I won't accuse you of such a thing again." He sealed his promise with a kiss that made her long for more, but he was not yet quite finished.

"If this is clean-slate night, love, would you be willing to tell me where you have been disappearing to so often and making me so infernally jealous?" He raised one eyebrow in a mocking gesture, but she knew he was very serious and she must tell him.

"Would you mind if I show you in the morning? It's a

little late to wander around upstairs with a branch of candles, but I found a little hideaway where no one ever goes. I went up there and dreamed I was back in Warwickshire, stealing off to some quiet place by a brook. You had the library where you could closet yourself with orders not to be disturbed, but I had nowhere I could go to be alone. The more unhappy I became, the more I needed to get away. Can you understand?"

He smiled, completely relieved of what had been a very grave concern. "Absolutely. Why didn't I realize that before? The first time we met you were just returning from a secret hideaway, weren't you? If you had told me, my love, I would have understood," he said earnestly. "You asked me the other day to take you home to Warwickshire. Do you still want to go?"

"Oh yes, please, Charles." Her face was filled with longing. "Could we, do you think?"

"Just as soon as the trial is over. It would be pointless to go before, as we'd only have to come back for it."

She gasped. "I'd forgotten about that. Will I have to testify against them?"

"Not if I can help it, my love. I believe John's evidence and my own will be sufficient to get them deported for life. I will not be satisfied with anything less."

Sir John was able to use his influence to persuade the magistrate to give an early hearing of the charges against the two kidnappers, and to save Emmeline the ordeal of having to testify in court. When it was over, Sir John came back for a celebration dinner for just the three of them and Grandmama. After they had finished eating, and the ladies' tea was brought in with the port, Emmeline asked the question she had been concerned about for some time.

"Did you ever find out if Mother and Agatha are still in town?" The question was addressed to Charles, but he looked across at Sir John and nodded.

"When I returned to the house where you were drugged, there was no sign that any of your family had ever been there. An old man lives in the basement and looks after the place. He said it had been rented out for some months, but the rent had been paid directly to the owner and he hadn't even met the tenants. The maid you described was probably a local, hired for a few days and then let go." He raised his eyebrows in silent question to Charles, who continued the story.

"We verified that they were back in Yorkshire, my dear, and came to the conclusion it was the best place for them to be. If you had been willing to have Agatha arrested . . ." he said, and Emmeline shook her head vehemently. "It would have been necessary for you to appear in court, and I was much against that. And there was nothing to prove that your mother ever had anything to do with the plot, though there is no doubt in my mind that it was she who urged Agatha's participation."

"Are you forbidding me to ever see them again, my lord?" Emmeline's face was tense, her eyes huge.

"No, my dear, but I wouldn't think it wise of you to contact them for some time, if ever. You have a forgiving nature, and I believe they were only used as pawns by Lord Barrow and Frobisher, if somewhat willing ones. But the decision is yours."

He turned to Sir John. "We leave for Warwickshire in the morning, to rusticate and get some color back in Emmeline's cheeks. We hope to see you there often when you've had your fill of the Season."

THEIR FIRST HOUSE party had been a large one, consisting mostly of family, as befitted such an important occasion. The guest of honor, now bearing the formidable names of John Charles Edward Carruthers, had been tucked into his crib despite his mild protests, and there was an atmosphere of celebration in the air. The proud grandfather, having made his first journey of any length in more than a year, conversed happily with Lady Poole.

"Knew her father well, you know, and she's the image of him," he told her. "Between you and me, I played not a small part in getting the two young people together. Made for each other right from the start, they were. Best thing I ever did."

Lady Poole's smile could easily have been taken for a grimace had it not been for the twinkle in her eyes. "Indeed, my lord, is that so? I like to feel that I played some part also in assuring their connubial bliss," she remarked with a chortle.

A SLENDER FIGURE dressed in a jacket and what appeared to be a narrow skirt slipped quietly out of the back door and entered the stables where Thunder was already saddled and waiting impatiently. Moving as one, horse and rider left the stables and set a fair pace, skirting the woods to the east of the house and across a meadow until a large oak came into view. Thunder gave a soft nicker.

"Do you want me to give you ten lengths, darling?"

The rider turned with a cry of delight, then lifted her head proudly. "Certainly not! On the count of three— one, two three!"

They raced neck and neck, neither giving the other quarter, until Thunder slowly inched forward and passed the tree just a foot ahead of the other horse.

Slowing, they headed for the nearby stream and Emmeline waited until Charles dismounted and tied his horse to a tree, then allowed him to assist her.

"You're still the best woman rider I've ever seen,

love," he murmured as they strolled toward the water, their arms entwined. "Also the best mother, and the best wife. And I am the luckiest man in all of England."

"I'm afraid I'm not the best hostess, though," she said ruefully, "but I just had to get away."

"I knew it, and I had Bart alerted to inform me the minute you asked for a horse. Don't ever change, Emmie, for I love you exactly as you are. I believe I always did, but hadn't the wit to realize it until I nearly lost you. I will forever be in John Barrington's debt."

"Mm. Me too, to everything you just said. But enough talk for now," Emmeline whispered, and turned into his arms, where her lips told of her love, and her happiness, more eloquently than any words.

About the Author

A native of Yorkshire, England, Irene Saunders spent a number of years exploring London while working for the U.S. Air Force there. A love of travel brought her to New York City, where she met her husband, Ray, then settled in Miami, Florida. She now lives in Port St. Lucie, Florida, dividing her time between writing, bookkeeping, gardening, needlepoint, and travel.

SIGNET REGENCY ROMANCE (0451)

FOLLIES OF THE HEART

- [ ] THE WOOD NYMPH by Mary Balogh (146506—$2.50)
- [ ] A CHANCE ENCOUNTER by Mary Balogh (140060—$2.50)
- [ ] THE DOUBLE WAGER by Mary Balogh (136179—$2.50)
- [ ] A MASKED DECEPTION by Mary Balogh (134052—$2.50)
- [ ] RED ROSE by Mary Balogh (141571—$2.50)
- [ ] THE TRYSTING PLACE by Mary Balogh (143000—$2.50)
- [ ] POOR RELATION by Marion Chesney (145917—$2.50)
- [ ] THE EDUCATION OF MISS PATTERSON by Marion Chesney (140052—$2.50)
- [ ] THE ORIGINAL MISS HONEYFORD by Marion Chesney (135660—$2.50)
- [ ] MARRIAGE MART by Norma Lee Clark (128168—$2.25)
- [ ] THE PERFECT MATCH by Norma Lee Clark (124839—$2.25)
- [ ] THE IMPULSIVE MISS PYMBROKE by Norma Lee Clark (132734—$2.50)
- [ ] CAPTAIN BLACK by Elizabeth Hewitt (131967—$2.50)
- [ ] MARRIAGE BY CONSENT by Elizabeth Hewitt (136152—$2.50)
- [ ] A SPORTING PROPOSITION by Elizabeth Hewitt (143515—$2.50)
- [ ] A MIND OF HER OWN by Anne McNeill (124820—$2.25)
- [ ] THE LUCKLESS ELOPEMENT by Dorothy Mack (129695—$2.25)
- [ ] THE BELEAGUERED LORD BOURNE by Michelle Kasey (140443—$2.50)

Prices slightly higher in Canada

Buy them at your local bookstore or use this convenient coupon for ordering.

NEW AMERICAN LIBRARY
P.O. Box 999, Bergenfield, New Jersey 07621

Please send me the books I have checked above. I am enclosing $_____
(please add $1.00 to this order to cover postage and handling). Send check or money order—no cash or C.O.D.'s. Prices and numbers are subject to change without notice.

Name_____

Address_____

City_____ State_____ Zip Code_____

Allow 4-6 weeks for delivery.
This offer is subject to withdrawal without notice.